SHORT
TAKES

YEARLING BOOKS/YOUNG YEARLINGS/YEARLING CLASSICS are designed especially to entertain and enlighten young people. Patricia Reilly Giff, consultant to this series, received her bachelor's degree from Marymount College and a master's degree in history from St. John's University. She holds a Professional Diploma in Reading and a Doctorate of Humane Letters from Hofstra University. She was a teacher and reading consultant for many years, and is the author of numerous books for young readers.

For a complete listing of all Yearling titles,
write to Dell Readers Service,
P.O. Box 1045,
South Holland, IL 60473.

SHORT TAKES

A Short Story Collection
for Young Readers

Selected by Elizabeth Segel

Illustrated by Jos. A. Smith

A Yearling Book

Published by
Dell Publishing
a division of
Bantam Doubleday Dell Publishing Group, Inc.
666 Fifth Avenue
New York, New York 10103

Four of the stories in this collection have been reprinted from other volumes:

"President Cleveland, Where Are You?" by Robert Cormier appeared in the collection *Eight Plus One* (Pantheon, 1980).

"On Shark's Tooth Beach" by E. L. Konigsburg appeared in *Throwing Shadows* (Atheneum, 1979).

"The Great Blackberry Pick" by Philippa Pearce appeared in *What the Neighbors Did and Other Stories* (Crowell, 1973).

"Shoes" by John Wideman appeared in *Ideas and Patterns in Literature III* (Harcourt, 1970). This volume has long been out of print.

Copyright © 1986 by Elizabeth Segel

Illustrations copyright © 1986 by Jos. A. Smith

The trademark Yearling® is registered in the U.S. Patent and Trademark Office.

The trademark Dell® is registered in the U.S. Patent and Trademark Office.

ISBN: 0-440-40581-5

Reprinted by arrangement with William Morrow & Company, Inc., on behalf of Lothrop, Lee & Shepard Books

Printed in the United States of America

February 1992

10 9 8 7 6 5 4 3 2 1

OPM

Contents

Introduction   vii

Tuesday of the Other June   2
   BY NORMA FOX MAZER

President Cleveland, Where Are You?   18
   BY ROBERT CORMIER

Last Summer   36
   BY TRICIA SPRINGSTUBB

On Shark's Tooth Beach   60
   BY E. L. KONIGSBURG

Splendor   84
   BY LOIS LOWRY

The Great Blackberry Pick   106
   BY PHILIPPA PEARCE

The Snakeskin Bag   122
   BY CONSTANCE C. GREENE

Shoes   130
   BY JOHN WIDEMAN

Your Mind Is a Mirror   136
   BY JOAN AIKEN

About the Authors   161

Introduction

I HAVE ALWAYS LOVED SHORT STORIES FOR THE VERY special pleasure they can provide—the pleasure of a complete story that can be experienced in a few minutes of reading time. Novels are wonderful, too, of course, and often I pick out a big book and look forward to spending days and weeks visiting a fictional world and getting to know the characters who live there. Yet there's nothing quite like a short story.

Because a short story can usually be read from start to finish all at once, it's ideal bedtime reading. If you start reading a novel at bedtime, you may end up lying awake wondering what is going to happen in the next exciting chapter, or stay up reading until late at night in order to find out. But you can read a whole short story at bedtime and still get a good night's sleep!

Beyond this practical advantage, the shortness of short stories gives them a special kind of impact. Because a short story must be told completely in a few hundred words, the best short story writers work hard to make every word count. A good short story has a concentrated, high-energy effect on the reader's feelings, because the writer has chosen each word and detail for its power to move us, to make us laugh or cry or understand.

Most of all, I love the way the best short stories highlight one brief experience that stands out from the sometimes boring wake-up, eat-breakfast, go-to-school routine of daily life.

When I was a child, one of my favorite toys was a kaleidoscope. I knew that it contained only a jumble of little colored pebbles, but when I looked through the eyepiece and slowly turned the long tube, brightly colored shapes at the far end tumbled and magically formed themselves into orderly, glowing patterns. For me, the successful short story does something very similar. From the confusion of life, it captures and focuses on a special moment, making it stand out as clearly and vividly as that pattern in which the kaleidoscope's tumbling shapes came to rest. When this happens, I suddenly understand something about life that I didn't see before—something painful perhaps, or funny, or beautiful ... something I will never forget.

Most of the writers whose stories appear in this book are best known for the longer books they have written for young readers. But they all share my enthusiasm for the short story and were happy to contribute to this collection. Like all good short story writers, they have preserved for us exciting or strange, funny or touching moments in the lives of ordinary people, before the kaleidoscope of life turns again and the clear, vivid pattern disappears.

Elizabeth Segel

Tuesday of the Other June

by Norma Fox Mazer

When you know you're supposed to act a certain way,
but everything inside you tells you to do just the op-
posite, it can be hard to get out of bed in the morning—
especially on Tuesday. . . .

"BE GOOD, BE GOOD, BE GOOD, BE GOOD, MY JUNIE," my mother sang as she combed my hair; a song, a story, a croon, a plea. "It's just you and me, two women alone in the world, June darling of my heart, we have enough troubles getting by, we surely don't need a single one more, so you keep your sweet self out of fighting and all that bad stuff. People can be little-hearted, but turn the other cheek, smile at the world, and the world'll surely smile back."

We stood in front of the mirror as she combed my hair, combed and brushed and smoothed. Her head came just above mine, she said when I grew another inch she'd stand on a stool to brush my hair. "I'm not giving up this pleasure!" And she laughed her long honey laugh.

My mother was April, my grandmother had been May, I was June. "And someday," said my mother, "you'll have a daughter of your own. What will you name her?"

"January!" I'd yell when I was little. "February! No, November!" My mother laughed her honey laugh. She had little emerald eyes that warmed me like the sun.

Every day when I went to school, she went to work. "Sometimes I stop what I'm doing," she said, "lay down my tools, and stop everything, because all I can think about is you. Wondering what you're doing and if you need me. Now, Junie, if anyone ever bothers you—"

3

"—I walk away, run away, come on home as fast as my feet will take me," I recited.

"Yes. You come to me. You just bring me your trouble, because I'm here on this earth to love you and take care of you."

I was safe with her. Still, sometimes I woke up at night and heard footsteps slowly creeping up the stairs. It wasn't my mother, she was asleep in the bed across the room, so it was robbers, thieves, and murderers, creeping slowly . . . slowly . . . slowly toward my bed.

I stuffed my hand into my mouth. If I screamed and woke her, she'd be tired at work tomorrow. The robbers and thieves filled the warm darkness and slipped across the floor more quietly than cats. Rigid under the covers, I stared at the shifting dark and bit my knuckles and never knew when I fell asleep again.

In the morning we sang in the kitchen. "Bill Grogan's GOAT! Was feelin' FINE! Ate three red shirts, right off the LINE!" I made sandwiches for our lunches, she made pancakes for breakfast, but all she ate was one pancake and a cup of coffee. "Gotta fly, can't be late."

I wanted to be rich and take care of her. She worked too hard, her pretty hair had gray in it that she joked about. "Someday," I said, "I'll buy you a real house and you'll never work in a pot factory again."

"Such delicious plans," she said. She checked

the windows to see if they were locked. "Do you have your key?"

I lifted it from the chain around my neck.

"And you'll come right home from school and—"

"—I won't light fires or let strangers into the house and I won't tell anyone on the phone that I'm here alone," I finished for her.

"I know, I'm just your old worrywart mother." She kissed me twice, once on each cheek. "But you are my June, my only June, the only June."

She was wrong, there was another June. I met her when we stood next to each other at the edge of the pool the first day of swimming class in the Community Center.

"What's your name?" She had a deep growly voice.

"June. What's yours?"

She stared at me. "June."

"We have the same name."

"No we don't. June is my name, and I don't give you permission to use it. Your name is Fish Eyes." She pinched me hard. "Got it, Fish Eyes?"

The next Tuesday, the Other June again stood next to me at the edge of the pool. "What's your name?"

"June."

"Wrong. Your—name—is—Fish—Eyes."

"June."

"Fish Eyes, you are really stupid." She shoved me into the pool.

5

The swimming teacher looked up, frowning, from her chart. "No one in the water yet."

Later, in the locker room, I dressed quickly and wrapped my wet suit in the towel. The Other June pulled on her jeans. "You guys see that bathing suit Fish Eyes was wearing? Her mother found it in a trash can."

"She did not!"

The Other June grabbed my fingers and twisted. "Where'd she find your bathing suit?"

"She bought it, let me go."

"Poor little stupid Fish Eyes is crying. Oh, boo hoo hoo, poor little Fish Eyes."

After that, everyone called me Fish Eyes. And every Tuesday, wherever I was, there was also the Other June—at the edge of the pool, in the pool, in the locker room. In the water, she swam alongside me, blowing and huffing, knocking into me. In the locker room, she stepped on my feet, pinched my arms, hid my blouse, and knotted my braids together. She had large square teeth, she was shorter than I was, but heavier, with bigger bones and square hands. If I met her outside on the street, carrying her bathing suit and towel, she'd walk toward me, smiling a square, friendly smile. "Oh well, if it isn't Fish Eyes." Then she'd punch me, *blam!* her whole solid weight hitting me.

I didn't know what to do about her. She was training me like a dog. After a few weeks of this, she only had to look at me, only had to growl, "I'm going to get you, Fish Eyes," for my heart to slink like a whipped dog down into my stomach. My arms were covered with bruises. When my mother noticed, I made up a story about tripping on the sidewalk.

My weeks were no longer Tuesday, Wednesday, Thursday, and so on. Tuesday was Awfulday. Wednesday was Badday. (The Tuesday bad feelings were still there.) Thursday was Betterday and Friday was Safeday. Saturday was Goodday, but Sunday was Toosoonday, and Monday—Monday was nothing but the day before Awfulday.

I tried to slow down time. Especially on the weekends, I stayed close by my mother, doing everything with her, shopping, cooking, cleaning, going to the laundromat. "Aw, sweetie, go play with your friends."

"No, I'd rather be with you." I wouldn't look at the clock or listen to the radio (they were always telling you the date and the time). I did special magic things to keep the day from going away, rapping my knuckles six times on the bathroom door six times a day and never, ever touching the chipped place on my bureau. But always I woke up to the day before Tuesday, and always, no matter how many times I circled the worn spot in the living-room rug or counted twenty-five cracks in the ceiling, Monday disappeared and once again it was Tuesday.

The Other June got bored with calling me Fish

Eyes. Buffalo Brain came next, but as soon as everyone knew that, she renamed me Turkey Nose.

Now at night it wasn't robbers creeping up the stairs, but the Other June, coming to torment me. When I finally fell asleep, I dreamed of kicking her, punching, biting, pinching. In the morning I remembered my dreams and felt brave and strong. And then I remembered all the things my mother had taught me and told me.

Be good, be good, be good, it's just us two women alone in the world . . . Oh, but if it weren't, if my father wasn't long gone, if we'd had someone else to fall back on, if my mother's mother and daddy weren't dead all these years, if my father's daddy wanted to know us instead of being glad to forget us—oh, then I would have punched the Other June with a frisky heart, I would have grabbed her arm at poolside and bitten her like the dog she had made of me.

One night, when my mother came home from work, she said, "Junie, listen to this. We're moving!"

Alaska, I thought. Florida. Arizona. Someplace far away and wonderful, someplace without the Other June.

"Wait till you hear this deal. We are going to be caretakers, troubleshooters for an eight-family apartment building. Fifty-six Blue Hill Street. Not janitors, we don't do any of the heavy work. April and June, Troubleshooters, Incorporated. If a tenant has a complaint or a problem, she comes to us and we either take care of it or call the janitor for service. And for that little bit of work, we get to live rent free!" She swept me around in a dance. "Okay? You like it? I do!"

So. Not anywhere else, really. All the same, maybe too far to go to swimming class? "Can we move right away? Today?"

"Gimme a break, sweetie. We've got to pack, do a thousand things. I've got to line up someone with a truck to help us. Six weeks, Saturday the fifteenth." She circled it on the calendar. It was the Saturday after the last day of swimming class.

Soon, we had boxes lying everywhere, filled with clothes and towels and glasses wrapped in newspaper. Bit by bit, we cleared the rooms, leaving only what we needed right now. The dining-room table staggered on a bunched-up rug, our bureaus inched toward the front door like patient cows. On the calendar in the kitchen, my mother marked off the days until we moved, but the only days I thought about were Tuesdays—Awfuldays. Nothing else was real except the too fast passing of time, moving toward each Tuesday . . . away from Tuesday . . . toward Tuesday. . . .

And it seemed to me that this would go on forever, that Tuesdays would come forever and I would be forever trapped by the side of the pool, the Other June whispering *Buffalo Brain Fish Eyes Turkey Nose* into my ear, while she ground her elbow into my side and smiled her square smile at the swimming teacher.

And then it ended. It was the last day of swimming class. The last Tuesday. We had all passed our tests and, as if in celebration, the Other June only pinched me twice. "And now," our swimming teacher said, "all of you are ready for the Advanced Class, which starts in just one month. I have a sign-up slip here. Please put your name down before you leave." Everyone but me crowded around. I went to the locker room and pulled on my clothes as fast as possible. The Other June burst through the door just as I was leaving. "Goodbye," I yelled, "good riddance to bad trash!" Before she could pinch me again, I ran past her and then ran all the way home, singing, "Goodbye ... goodbye ... goodbye, good riddance to bad trash!"

Later, my mother carefully untied the blue ribbon around my swimming class diploma. "Look at this! Well, isn't this wonderful! You are on your way, you might turn into an Olympic swimmer, you never know what life will bring."

"I don't want to take more lessons."

"Oh, sweetie, it's great to be a good swimmer." But then, looking into my face, she said, "No, no, no, don't worry, you don't have to."

10

The next morning, I woke up hungry for the first time in weeks. No more swimming class. No more Baddays and Awfuldays. No more Tuesdays of the Other June. In the kitchen, I made hot cocoa to go with my mother's corn muffins. "It's Wednesday, Mom," I said, stirring the cocoa. "My favorite day."

"Since when?"

"Since this morning." I turned on the radio so I could hear the announcer tell the time, the temperature, and the day.

Thursday for breakfast I made cinnamon toast, Friday my mother made pancakes, and on Saturday, before we moved, we ate the last slices of bread and cleaned out the peanut butter jar.

"Some breakfast," Tilly said. "Hello, you must be June." She shook my hand. She was a friend of my mother's from work, she wore big hoop earrings, sandals, and a skirt as dazzling as a rainbow. She came in a truck with John to help us move our things.

John shouted cheerfully at me, "So you're moving." An enormous man with a face covered with little brown bumps. Was he afraid his voice wouldn't travel the distance from his mouth to my ear? "You looking at my moles?" he shouted, and he heaved our big green flowered chair down the stairs. "Don't worry, they don't bite. Ha, ha, ha!" Behind him came my mother and Tilly balancing a bureau between them, and behind them I carried a lamp and the round, flowered Mexican tray that was my mother's favorite. She had found it at a garage sale and said it was as close to foreign travel as we would ever get.

The night before, we had loaded our car, stuffing in bags and boxes until there was barely room for the two of us. But it was only when we were in the car, when we drove past Abdo's Grocery, where they always gave us credit, when I turned for a last look at our street—it was only then that I understood we were truly going to live somewhere else, in another apartment, in another place mysteriously called Blue Hill Street.

Tilly's truck followed our car.

"Oh, I'm so excited," my mother said. She laughed. "You'd think we were going across the country."

Our old car wheezed up a long steep hill. Blue Hill Street. I looked from one side to the other, trying to see everything.

My mother drove over the crest of the hill. "And now—ta da!—our new home."

"Which house? Which one?" I looked out the window and what I saw was the Other June. She was sprawled on the stoop of a pink house, lounging back on her elbows, legs outspread, her jaws working on a wad of gum. I slid down into the seat, but it was too late. I was sure she had seen me.

My mother turned into a driveway next to a big white building with a tiny porch. She leaned on the steering wheel. "See that window there, that's our living-room window . . . and that one over there, that's your bedroom. . . ."

We went into the house, down a dim cool hall. In our new apartment, the wooden floors clicked under our shoes, and my mother showed me everything. Her voice echoed in the empty rooms. I followed her around in a daze. Had I imagined seeing the Other June? Maybe I'd seen another girl who looked like her. A double. That could happen.

"Ho yo, where do you want this chair?" John appeared in the doorway. We brought in boxes and bags and beds and stopped only to eat pizza and drink orange juice from the carton.

"June's so quiet, do you think she'll adjust all right?" I heard Tilly say to my mother.

"Oh, definitely. She'll make a wonderful adjustment. She's just getting used to things."

But I thought that if the Other June lived on the same street as I did, I would never get used to things.

That night I slept in my own bed, with my own pillow and blanket, but with floors that creaked in strange voices and walls with cracks I didn't recognize. I didn't feel either happy or unhappy. It was as if I were waiting for something.

Monday, when the principal of Blue Hill Street

13

School left me in Mr. Morrisey's classroom, I knew what I'd been waiting for. In that room full of strange kids, there was one person I knew. She smiled her square smile, raised her hand, and said, "She can sit next to me, Mr. Morrisey."

"Very nice of you, June M. Okay, June T, take your seat. I'll try not to get you two Junes mixed up."

I sat down next to her. She pinched my arm. "Good riddance to bad trash," she mocked.

I was back in the Tuesday swimming class only now it was worse, because everyday would be Awfulday. The pinching had already started. Soon, I knew, on the playground and in the halls, kids would pass me, grinning. "Hiya, Fish Eyes."

The Other June followed me around during recess that day, droning in my ear, "You are my slave, you must do everything I say, I am your master, say it, say, 'Yes, master, you are my master.'"

I pressed my lips together, clapped my hands over my ears, but without hope. Wasn't it only a matter of time before I said the hateful words?

"How was school?" my mother said that night.

"Okay."

She put a pile of towels in a bureau drawer. "Try not to be sad about missing your old friends, sweetie, there'll be new ones."

The next morning, the Other June was waiting

for me when I left the house. "Did your mother get you that blouse in the garbage dump?" She butted me, shoving me against a tree. "Don't you speak anymore, Fish Eyes?" Grabbing my chin in her hands, she pried open my mouth. "Oh, ha ha, I thought you lost your tongue."

We went on to school. I sank down into my seat, my head on my arms. "June T, are you all right?" Mr. Morrisey asked. I nodded. My head was almost too heavy to lift.

The Other June went to the pencil sharpener. Round and round she whirled the handle. Walking back, looking at me, she held the three sharp pencils like three little knives.

Someone knocked on the door. Mr. Morrisey went out into the hall. Paper planes burst into the air, flying from desk to desk. Someone turned on a transistor radio. And the Other June, coming closer, smiled and licked her lips like a cat sleepily preparing to gulp down a mouse.

I remembered my dream of kicking her, punching, biting her like a dog.

Then my mother spoke quickly in my ear: *Turn the other cheek, my Junie, smile at the world and the world'll surely smile back.*

But I had turned the other cheek and it was slapped. I had smiled and the world hadn't smiled back. I couldn't run home as fast as my feet would take me, I had to stay in school—and in school there was the Other June. Every morning, there would be the Other June, and every afternoon, and every day, all day, there would be the Other June.

She frisked down the aisle, stabbing the pencils in the air toward me. A boy stood up on his desk and bowed. "My fans," he said, "I greet you." My arm twitched and throbbed, as if the Other June's pencils had already poked through the skin. She came closer, smiling her Tuesday smile.

"No," I whispered, "no." The word took wings and flew me to my feet, in front of the Other June. "Noooooo." It flew out of my mouth into her surprised face.

The boy on the desk turned toward us. "You said something, my devoted fans?"

"No," I said to the Other June. "Oh, no! No. No. No. No more." I pushed away the hand that held the pencils.

The Other June's eyes opened, popped wide like the eyes of somebody in a cartoon. It made me laugh. The boy on the desk laughed, and then the other kids were laughing, too.

"No," I said again, because it felt so good to say it. "No, no, no, no." I leaned toward the Other June, put my finger against her chest. Her cheeks turned red, she squawked something—it sounded like "Eeeraaghyou!"—and she stepped back. She stepped away from me.

The door banged, the airplanes disappeared, and

Mr. Morrisey walked to his desk. "Okay. Okay. Let's get back to work. Kevin Clark, how about it?" Kevin jumped off the desk and Mr. Morrisey picked up a piece of chalk. "All right, class—" He stopped and looked at me and the Other June. "You two Junes, what's going on there?"

I tried it again. My finger against her chest. Then the words. "No—more." And she stepped back another step. I sat down at my desk.

"June M," Mr. Morrisey said.

She turned around, staring at him with that big-eyed cartoon look. After a moment she sat down at her desk with a loud slapping sound.

Even Mr. Morrisey laughed.

And sitting at my desk, twirling my braids, I knew this was the last Tuesday of the Other June.

President Cleveland, Where Are You?

by Robert Cormier

A bubble gum card or a baseball glove can be the most important thing in the world, when you want it so badly you'd give anything to get it. But nothing is simple, not even getting what you want....

THAT WAS THE AUTUMN OF THE COWBOY CARDS—Buck Jones and Tom Tyler and Hoot Gibson and especially Ken Maynard. The cards were available in those five-cent packages of gum: pink sticks, three together, covered with a sweet white powder. You couldn't blow bubbles with that particular gum, but it couldn't have mattered less. The cowboy cards were important—the pictures of those rock-faced men with eyes of blue steel.

On those windswept, leaf-tumbling afternoons we gathered after school on the sidewalk in front of Lemire's Drugstore, across from St. Jude's Parochial School, and we swapped and bargained and matched for the cards. Because a Ken Maynard serial was playing at the Globe every Saturday afternoon, he was the most popular cowboy of all, and one of his cards was worth at least ten of any other kind. Rollie Tremaine had a treasure of thirty or so, and he guarded them jealously. He'd match you for the other cards, but he risked his Ken Maynards only when the other kids threatened to leave him out of the competition altogether.

You could almost hate Rollie Tremaine. In the first place, he was the only son of Auguste Tremaine, who operated the Uptown Dry Goods Store, and he did not live in a tenement but in a big white birthday cake of a house on Laurel Street. He was too fat to be effective in the football games between the Frenchtown Tigers and the North Side Knights, and he made us constantly aware of the jingle of coins in his pockets. He was able to stroll into Lemire's and casually select a quarter's worth of cowboy cards while the rest of us watched, aching with envy.

Once in a while I earned a nickel or dime by running errands or washing windows for blind old Mrs. Belander, or by finding pieces of copper, brass, and other valuable metals at the dump and selling them to the junkman. The coins clutched in my hand, I would race to Lemire's to buy a cowboy card or two, hoping that Ken Maynard would stare boldly out at me as I opened the pack. At one time, before a disastrous matching session with Roger Lussier (my best friend, except where the cards were involved), I owned five Ken Maynards and considered myself a millionaire, of sorts.

One week I was particularly lucky; I had spent two afternoons washing floors for Mrs. Belander and received a quarter. Because my father had worked a full week at the shop, where a rush order for fancy combs had been received, he allotted my brothers and sisters and me an extra dime along with the usual ten cents for the Saturday-afternoon movie. Setting aside the movie fare, I found myself with a bonus of thirty-five cents, and I then planned to put Rollie Tremaine to shame the following Monday afternoon.

Monday was the best day to buy the cards because the candy man stopped at Lemire's every Monday morning to deliver the new assortments. There was nothing more exciting in the world than a fresh batch of card boxes. I rushed home from school that day and hurriedly changed my clothes, eager to set off for the store. As I burst through the doorway, letting the screen door slam behind me, my brother Armand blocked my way.

He was fourteen, three years older than I, and a freshman at Monument High School. He had recently become a stranger to me in many ways—indifferent to such matters as cowboy cards and the Frenchtown Tigers—and he carried himself with a mysterious dignity that was fractured now and then when his voice began shooting off in all directions like some kind of vocal fireworks.

"Wait a minute, Jerry," he said. "I want to talk to you." He motioned me out of earshot of my mother, who was busy supervising the usual after-school skirmish in the kitchen.

I sighed with impatience. In recent months Armand had become a figure of authority, siding with my father and mother occasionally. As the oldest son he sometimes took advantage of his age and experience to issue rules and regulations.

"How much money have you got?" he whispered.

"You in some kind of trouble?" I asked, excitement rising in me as I remembered the blackmail plot of a movie at the Globe a month before.

He shook his head in annoyance. "Look," he said, "it's Pa's birthday tomorrow. I think we ought to chip in and buy him something . . ."

I reached into my pocket and caressed the coins. "Here," I said carefully, pulling out a nickel. "If we all give a nickel we should have enough to buy him something pretty nice."

He regarded me with contempt. "Rita already gave me fifteen cents, and I'm throwing in a quarter. Albert handed over a dime—all that's left of his birthday money. Is that all you can do—a nickel?"

"Aw, come on," I protested. "I haven't got a single Ken Maynard left, and I was going to buy some cards this afternoon."

"Ken Maynard!" he snorted. "Who's more important—him or your father?"

His question was unfair because he knew that there was no possible choice—"my father" had to be the only answer. My father was a huge man who believed in the things of the spirit, although my mother often maintained that the spirits he believed in came in bottles. He had worked at the Monument Comb Shop since the age of fourteen; his booming laugh—or grumble—greeted us each night when he returned from the factory. A steady worker when the shop had enough work, he

22

quickened with gaiety on Friday nights and week-ends, a bottle of beer at his elbow, and he was fond of making long speeches about the good things in life. In the middle of the Depression, for instance, he paid cash for a piano, of all things, and insisted that my twin sisters, Yolande and Yvette, take lessons once a week.

I took a dime from my pocket and handed it to Armand.

"Thanks, Jerry," he said. "I hate to take your last cent."

"That's all right," I replied, turning away and consoling myself with the thought that twenty cents was better than nothing at all.

When I arrived at Lemire's I sensed disaster in the air. Roger Lussier was kicking disconsolately at a tin can in the gutter, and Rollie Tremaine sat sullenly on the steps in front of the store.

"Save your money," Roger said. He had known about my plans to splurge on the cards.

"What's the matter?" I asked.

"There's no more cowboy cards," Rollie Tremaine said. "The company's not making any more."

"They're going to have President cards," Roger said, his face twisting with disgust. He pointed to the store window. "Look!"

A placard in the window announced: "Attention, Boys. Watch for the New Series. Presidents of the United States. Free in Each 5-Cent Package of Caramel Chew."

"President cards?" I asked, dismayed.

I read on: "Collect a Complete Set and Receive an Official Imitation Major League Baseball Glove, Embossed with Lefty Grove's Autograph."

Glove or no glove, who could become excited about Presidents, of all things?

Rollie Tremaine stared at the sign. "Benjamin Harrison, for crying out loud," he said. "Why would I want Benjamin Harrison when I've got twenty-two Ken Maynards?"

I felt the warmth of guilt creep over me. I jingled the coins in my pocket, but the sound was hollow. No more Ken Maynards to buy.

"I'm going to buy a Mr. Goodbar," Rollie Tremaine decided.

I was without appetite, indifferent even to a Baby Ruth, which was my favorite. I thought of how I had betrayed Armand and, worst of all, my father.

"I'll see you after supper," I called over my shoulder to Roger as I hurried away toward home. I took the shortcut behind the church, although it involved leaping over a tall wooden fence, and I zigzagged recklessly through Mr. Thibodeau's garden, trying to outrace my guilt. I pounded up the steps and into the house, only to learn that Armand had already taken Yolande and

Yvette uptown to shop for the birthday present.

I pedaled my bike furiously through the streets, ignoring the indignant horns of automobiles as I sliced through the traffic. Finally I saw Armand and my sisters emerge from the Monument Men's Shop. My heart sank when I spied the long, slim package that Armand was holding.

"Did you buy the present yet?" I asked, although I knew it was too late.

"Just now. A blue tie," Armand said. "What's the matter?"

"Nothing," I replied, my chest hurting.

He looked at me for a long moment. At first his eyes were hard, but then they softened. He smiled at me, almost sadly, and touched my arm. I turned away from him because I felt naked and exposed.

"It's all right," he said gently. "Maybe you've learned something." The words were gentle, but they held a curious dignity, the dignity remaining even when his voice suddenly cracked on the last syllable.

I wondered what was happening to me, because I did not know whether to laugh or cry.

Sister Angela was amazed when, a week before Christmas vacation, everybody in the class submitted a history essay worthy of a high mark—in some cases as high as A-minus. (Sister Angela did not believe that anyone in the world ever deserved an A.) She never learned—or at least she never let on that she knew—we all had become experts on the Presidents because of the cards we purchased at Lemire's. Each card contained a picture of a President, and on the reverse side, a summary of his career. We looked at those cards so often that the biographies imprinted themselves on our minds without effort. Even our street-corner conversations were filled with such information as the fact that James Madison was called "The Father of the Constitution," or that John Adams had intended to become a minister.

The President cards were a roaring success and the cowboy cards were quickly forgotten. In the first place we did not receive gum with the cards, but a kind of chewy caramel. The caramel could be tucked into a corner of your mouth, bulging your cheek in much the same manner as wads of tobacco bulged the mouths of baseball stars. In the second place the competition for collecting the cards was fierce and frustrating—fierce because everyone was intent on being the first to send away for a baseball glove and frustrating because although there were only thirty-two Presidents, including Franklin Delano Roosevelt, the variety at Lemire's was at a minimum. When the deliveryman left the boxes of cards at the store each Monday, we often discovered that one entire box was devoted to a single President—two weeks in a row the boxes contained nothing but Abraham Lincolns. One week Roger Lussier and I were the heroes of Frenchtown. We journeyed on our bicycles to the North Side, engaged three boys in a matching bout and returned with five new Presidents, including Chester Alan Arthur, who up to that time had been missing.

Perhaps to sharpen our desire, the card company sent a sample glove to Mr. Lemire, and it dangled, orange and sleek, in the window. I was half sick with longing, thinking of my old glove at home, which I had inherited from Armand. But Rollie Tremaine's desire for the glove outdistanced my own. He even got Mr. Lemire to agree to give the glove in the window to the first person to get a complete set of cards, so that precious time wouldn't be wasted waiting for the postman.

We were delighted at Rollie Tremaine's frustration, especially since he was only a substitute player for the Tigers. Once after spending fifty cents on cards—all of which turned out to be Calvin Coolidge—he threw them to the ground, pulled some dollar bills out of his pocket and said, "The heck with it. I'm going to buy a glove!"

"Not that glove," Roger Lussier said. "Not a glove with Lefty Grove's autograph. Look what it says at the bottom of the sign."

We all looked, although we knew the words by heart: "This Glove Is Not For Sale Anywhere."

Rollie Tremaine scrambled to pick up the cards from the sidewalk, pouting more than ever. After that he was quietly obsessed with the Presidents, hugging the cards close to his chest and refusing to tell us how many more he needed to complete his set.

I too was obsessed with the cards, because they had become things of comfort in a world that had suddenly grown dismal. After Christmas a layoff at the shop had thrown my father out of work. He received no paycheck for four weeks, and the only income we had was from Armand's after-school job at the Blue and White Grocery Store—a job he lost finally when business dwindled as the layoff continued.

Although we had enough food and clothing— my father's credit had always been good, a matter of pride with him—the inactivity made my father restless and irritable. He did not drink any beer at all, and laughed loudly, but not convincingly, after gulping down a glass of water and saying, "Lent came early this year." The twins fell sick and went to the hospital to have their tonsils removed. My father was confident that he would return to work eventually and pay off his debts, but he seemed to age before our eyes.

When orders again were received at the comb shop and he returned to work, another disaster occurred, although I was the only one aware of it. Armand fell in love.

I discovered his situation by accident, when I happened to pick up a piece of paper that had fallen to the floor in the bedroom he and I shared. I frowned at the paper, puzzled.

"Dear Sally, When I look into your eyes the world stands still . . ."

The letter was snatched from my hands before I finished reading it.

"What's the big idea, snooping around?" Armand asked, his face crimson. "Can't a guy have any privacy?"

He had never mentioned privacy before. "It was on the floor," I said. "I didn't know it was a letter. Who's Sally?"

He flung himself across the bed. "You tell anybody and I'll muckalize you," he threatened. "Sally Knowlton."

Nobody in Frenchtown had a name like Knowlton.

"A girl from the North Side?" I asked, incredulous.

He rolled over and faced me, anger in his eyes, and a kind of despair too.

"What's the matter with that? Think she's too good for me?" he asked. "I'm warning you, Jerry, if you tell anybody . . ."

"Don't worry," I said. Love had no particular place in my life; it seemed an unnecessary waste of time. And a girl from the North Side was so remote that for all practical purposes she did not

29

exist. But I was curious. "What are you writing her a letter for? Did she leave town, or something?"

"She hasn't left town," he answered. "I wasn't going to send it. I just felt like writing to her."

I was glad that I had never become involved with love—love that brought desperation to your eyes, that caused you to write letters you did not plan to send. Shrugging with indifference, I began to search in the closet for the old baseball glove. I found it on the shelf, under some old sneakers. The webbing was torn and the padding gone. I thought of the sting I would feel when a sharp grounder slapped into the glove, and I winced.

"You tell anybody about me and Sally and I'll—"

"I know. You'll muckalize me."

I did not divulge his secret and often shared his agony, particularly when he sat at the supper table and left my mother's special butterscotch pie untouched. I had never realized before how terrible love could be. But my compassion was short-lived because I had other things to worry about: report cards due at Eastertime; the loss of income from old Mrs. Belander, who had gone to live with a daughter in Boston; and, of course, the Presidents.

Because a stalemate had been reached, the President cards were the dominant force in our lives— mine, Roger Lussier's and Rollie Tremaine's. For three weeks, as the baseball season approached, each of us had a complete set—complete except for one President, Grover Cleveland. Each time a box of cards arrived at the store we hurriedly bought them (as hurriedly as our funds allowed) and tore off the wrappers, only to be confronted by James Monroe or Martin Van Buren or someone else. But never Grover Cleveland, never the man who had been the twenty-second *and* the twenty-fourth President of the United States. We argued about Grover Cleveland. Should he be placed between Chester Alan Arthur and Benjamin Harrison as the twenty-second President or did he belong between Benjamin Harrison and William McKinley as the twenty-fourth President? Was the card company playing fair? Roger Lussier brought up a horrifying possibility—did we need *two* Grover Clevelands to complete the set?

Indignant, we stormed Lemire's and protested to the harassed store owner, who had long since vowed never to stock a new series. Muttering angrily, he searched his bills and receipts for a list of rules.

"All right," he announced. "Says here you only need one Grover Cleveland to finish the set. Now get out, all of you, unless you've got money to spend."

Outside the store, Rollie Tremaine picked up an empty tobacco tin and scaled it across the street. "Boy," he said. "I'd give five dollars for a Grover Cleveland."

When I returned home I found Armand sitting on the piazza steps, his chin in his hands. His mood of dejection mirrored my own, and I sat down beside him. We did not say anything for a while.

"Want to throw the ball around?" I asked.

He sighed, not bothering to answer.

"You sick?" I asked.

He stood up and hitched up his trousers, pulled at his ear and finally told me what the matter was—there was a big dance next week at the high school, the Spring Promenade, and Sally had asked him to be her escort.

I shook my head at the folly of love. "Well, what's so bad about that?"

"How can I take Sally to a fancy dance?" he asked desperately. "I'd have to buy her a corsage ... And my shoes are practically falling apart. Pa's got too many worries now to buy me new shoes or give me money for flowers for a girl."

I nodded in sympathy. "Yeah," I said. "Look at me. Baseball time is almost here, and all I've got is that old glove. And no Grover Cleveland card yet ..."

"Grover Cleveland?" he asked. "They've got some of those up on the North Side. Some kid was telling me there's a store that's got them. He says they're looking for Warren G. Harding."

"Holy Smoke!" I said. "I've got an extra Warren

G. Harding!" Pure joy sang in my veins. I ran to my bicycle, swung into the seat—and found that the front tire was flat.

"I'll help you fix it," Armand said.

Within half an hour I was at the North Side Drugstore, where several boys were matching cards on the sidewalk. Silently but blissfully I shouted: President Grover Cleveland, here I come!

After Armand had left for the dance, all dressed up as if it were Sunday, the small green box containing the corsage under his arm, I sat on the railing of the piazza, letting my feet dangle. The neighborhood was quiet because the Frenchtown Tigers were at Daggett's Field, practicing for the first baseball game of the season.

I thought of Armand and the ridiculous expression on his face when he'd stood before the mirror in the bedroom. I'd avoided looking at his new black shoes. "Love," I muttered.

Spring had arrived in a sudden stampede of apple blossoms and fragrant breezes. Windows had been thrown open and dust mops had banged on the sills all day long as the women busied themselves with housecleaning. I was puzzled by my lethargy. Wasn't spring supposed to make everything bright and gay?

I turned at the sound of footsteps on the stairs. Roger Lussier greeted me with a sour face.

"I thought you were practicing with the Tigers," I said.

"Rollie Tremaine," he said. "I just couldn't stand him." He slammed his fist against the railing. "Jeez, why did *he* have to be the one to get a Grover Cleveland? You should see him showing off. He won't let anybody even touch that glove . . ."

I felt like Benedict Arnold and knew that I had to confess what I had done.

"Roger," I said, "I got a Grover Cleveland card up on the North Side. I sold it to Rollie Tremaine for five dollars."

"Are you crazy?" he asked.

"I needed that five dollars. It was an—an emergency."

"Boy!" he said, looking down at the ground and shaking his head. "What did you have to do a thing like that for?"

I watched him as he turned away and began walking down the stairs.

"Hey, Roger!" I called.

He squinted up at me as if I were a stranger, someone he'd never seen before.

"What?" he asked, his voice flat.

"I had to do it," I said. "Honest."

He didn't answer. He headed toward the fence, searching for the board we had loosened to give us a secret passage.

34

I thought of my father and Armand and Rollie Tremaine and Grover Cleveland and wished that I could go away someplace far away. But there was no place to go.

Roger found the loose slat in the fence and slipped through. I felt betrayed; weren't you supposed to feel good when you did something fine and noble?

A moment later two hands gripped the top of the fence and Roger's face appeared. "Was it a real emergency?" he yelled.

"A real one!" I called. "Something important!"

His face dropped from sight and his voice reached me across the yard: "All right."

"See you tomorrow!" I yelled.

I swung my legs over the railing again. The gathering dusk began to soften the sharp edges of the fence, the rooftops, the distant church steeple. I sat there a long time, waiting for the good feeling to come.

Last Summer

by Tricia Springstubb

Suddenly everything is changing, and everyone else is on a different, faster track. Even if you don't want to go with them, it's hard to be left behind....

ON THE LAST DAY OF SIXTH GRADE EUNICE GOTTLIEB stared out the window of her classroom. It was a hot, blue, glorious day, which made the fact that she felt absolutely terrible all the more ridiculous. This was a day you were supposed to look forward to! Onward, upward, et cetera! If only the windows of her classroom didn't give directly onto the front lawn of the junior high. If only for weeks and weeks now she hadn't had to watch those seventh, eighth, and ninth graders going in and out. Speak of the devil—here they came now. When the last bell rang over there they flew out as if propelled by some inner explosion, and you could tell that if a measly sixth grader got in their way it would be just too bad for her. Junior-high girls wore makeup and somehow made their hair fluffy. They settled themselves into tight, impenetrable little groups, and they checked each other out. From head to foot. Inside out. Eunice saw the girls who had to walk home alone hurrying along with their heads down, trying to get out of sight as quickly as possible.

Oh God.

Holding an already ravaged pencil, she began to chew on it furiously. Her big sister, Millie, liked to tell her this habit caused lead poisoning, and that was why Eunice was so feebleminded. To think that Eunice had once considered Millie her life's greatest affliction. Little had she known what real trouble was.

Eunice's best friend, Joy McKenzie, came and stood beside her. They were supposed to be cleaning out their desks, but Joy's was, of course, already immaculate. Observing Eunice's weak-kneed state, she said, "Come on. Don't tell me you're worrying again."

"All right. I won't tell you."

"What are you afraid of? They're just kids!"

"You know that's not true."

Joy squinted out the window. "Two legs, two arms, backpacks, and mouths full of gum—they're certainly not hippopotami."

Eunice waved her pencil, ignoring Joy's look of disgust at it. "We hardly know any of them! Next year we'll be in classes with kids we've never laid eyes on before. Sixty-six point six percent of the school will be older than us! On a scale of zero to ten, we'll be minus fifteen! Joy, we'll be the youngest, plus—" she gulped—"we'll be among absolute strangers!"

"Egad! I keep telling you, that's what's so great about it!" Joy tossed her long, gleaming, butter-scotch-colored hair. "Junior high is a fresh start. This dumb class of ours—we've been together since kindergarten. We know each other backwards and forwards." She lowered her voice, as Mrs. Schwark raised an eyebrow. "Everyone knows Priscilla Berger is world champion blabbermouth, Mona Mahoney is afraid of her own shadow, Reggie Ackeroyd is a spoiled brat, you and I would swallow boiling oil for each other. . . . Admit it! Things have gotten positively incestuous."

That was one of those words Eunice couldn't have pronounced without a choking spasm and that Joy could drop with aplomb. It was true: Joy was no cowerer. She was quite capable of viewing junior high as an adventure, and over the past few weeks had tried to convince Eunice to feel the same way. Eunice, however, couldn't help looking out at those seventh, eighth, and ninth graders the way someone in a leaky boat would regard a river full of piranhas. When they smiled all she saw was teeth.

"But Joy, there's something nice about knowing where you stand. I mean—how do we know we'll fit in?"

"Fit in? What are we, puzzle pieces? We're individuals! Now stop chewing that pencil and come on away from this window—I'm starting to melt. Egad." She took a horrified sniff at her armpit. "I'm actually sweating."

Joy had been wearing antiperspirant for some time now. She'd had no trouble convincing her mother to let her, whereas Mrs. Gottlieb had laughed and told Eunice not to be silly. There was positively no chance that next year some eighth or ninth grader would sneak up behind Joy and announce "Beeeee-ohhhhh!" loudly enough to make the entire hallway lapse into mass hysterics. It occurred to Eunice that as long as she stayed best friends with Joy, she really had little to fear. And since their friendship was as unquestionable a force as gravity . . . Just think of all they'd been through together! Losing their front teeth, getting chicken pox, joining Girl Scouts, quitting Girl Scouts, Joy's dance recitals (Eunice in the front row every time), Eunice's threats to disown her family (Joy never teasing when she relented), hitchhiking to Akron to see the Rolling Stones, getting punished for hitchhiking to Akron to see the Rolling Stones—if Eunice were to make a list entitled Memorable Events of My Life, Joy would have been present at every one.

Across the room Reggie Ackeroyd, skinny as a dragonfly, was complaining to Mrs. Schwark that she was going to have to spend the next two weeks with her father, and he was taking her to France.

"*I* want to go to Disney World. I've already been to Europe *twice*," she whined, "and it's *yucky*."

Priscilla Berger was blabbing on and on as usual, and as usual no one but mousy little Mona Mahoney was paying the slightest attention. Looking around the room Eunice decided that Joy was probably right: the air had grown decidedly stale. It was, after all, time for a change. As her father said about aging: I prefer it to the alternative.

Eunice gathered herself up. She tossed out all her mutilated pencils and handed in the rest of her books. She bid Mrs. Schwark goodbye and, with Joy, as ever, at her side, marched out the door. I am, she told herself, prepared to begin a new life.

For the first week or two of vacation Joy and Eunice followed their usual routine, getting together in the early afternoon, after Joy's dance or tennis or cello lesson, and deciding what to do. They rode no-handed down Cedar Hill; they lounged in the air-conditioned library reading magazines; they lay under Eunice's plum tree drinking pop and talking. They each got a second hole pierced in their left ears. Once or twice a week they went to the town pool. Eunice had never much liked going there—she preferred the lake—and this year especially she disliked it. The pool was a prime junior-high hangout and Eunice, though assuring herself she was ready for seventh grade, was definitely not ready to be observed in a bathing suit. Up until recently she'd had a more or less friendly feeling toward her body—it got her where she wanted to go and only rarely needed repairs—but now she saw that it was convex and concave in all the wrong places, and showed no signs of changing. Totally inadequate. That was what those junior-high kids with their piercing scalpel-eyes could do: make you feel your own body was a traitor. When they went to the pool Eunice kept her T-shirt on as long as possible. She jumped in the water only when baking on the concrete became unbearable, and as soon as she got out she pulled her shirt back on. Joy, on the other hand, spent all her time on the high dive. She loved diving almost as much as she did dancing. "I guess I just enjoy defying gravity," she sighed.

One afternoon as Eunice huddled in her T-shirt, pretending to do a crossword puzzle but really eyeing the junior-high crowd that had commandeered one whole half of the poolside, she saw a boy detach himself from the crowd and come sit by the ladder across from the diving board. He was tall, with dark eyes and careless, tangled hair and the kind of honeyish tan that some blonds get. Joy was climbing up the high dive, and Eunice thought idly that the boy looked like one of those that hovered in the background of Cover Girl ads—so handsome you just knew he couldn't have an original thought in his head.

Up on the high dive Joy paused, surveying the earthbound world. She gave a small, expert bounce and came sailing down, slipping into the water with just the faintest whisper of a *whoosh*. Though Eunice had viewed this performance dozens of times, she still felt like applauding. In another era, Eunice knew, Joy would have been called A Paragon of Grace.

Joy surfaced and shook her head, sending diamond-bright drops of water flying. She was across the pool in three strokes, swinging herself up the ladder—and stumbling. Joy never stumbled. But then she'd never had a boy with eyes like that staring up into her face, either.

Eunice watched Joy walk back around and dive again. The boy sat very still, but somehow like a coiled-up spring. As Joy swam across and climbed the ladder he didn't take his eyes off her. Eunice felt a shiver up her spine, though her undeodoranted armpits were dripping.

Joy climbed the high dive once more, gave that small, businesslike bounce, and then—how did she do it? This time she seemed to drift down through the air in slow motion, as if she were an instant replay on *Wide World of Sports* or a magnolia petal blown loose in the breeze. There was only the barest ripple where she disappeared into the sky-blue water.

Eunice began to chew on her pencil.

This time when Joy climbed out she came straight to Eunice. Over her shoulder Eunice could see the boy turn to watch them. His eyes were like black stars.

In a voice uncharacteristically out of breath, Joy said, "That's enough."

But the next day she was at Eunice's early, already in her swimsuit.

"We went to the pool yesterday," said Eunice uneasily.

"It's too hot to do anything else."

"I thought we could go to the matinee at World East. It'll be arctic in there."

"Egad, Eu, stop whining. You sound like Reggie Ackeroyd. Air-conditioning is unhealthy. Let's go."

Eunice had to pedal hard to keep up with Joy, and by the time they reached the pool she was one big bucket of sweat. Hugging her armpits to her sides, she followed Joy out of the locker room— and saw the boy, sitting with a group of boys and girls, get up at once and come to sit by the ladder.

Eunice took a quick dip and then spread her towel next to Joy's, dropped in a hurried heap. One of the boy's friends yelled something to him and he turned his head just long enough to call something back. The friend pretended to fall down laughing.

"What a show-off!" screeched someone in Eunice's ear, just as Joy dove. It was Reggie Ackeroyd, yanking on the ridiculous marmalade-colored ponytail that spouted from the top of her bony head. "Does she think she's the only one in the world who can dive like that?"

Joy climbed out of the water and Eunice realized she was holding her breath, waiting for the boy to do something.

"*I* had private diving lessons last year." Reggie, who was one of the most emaciated people Eunice had ever seen, pulled on her ponytail. "But you won't catch *me* showing off like that! Want to see my waterproof watch? It's from Paris."

For the first time Joy looked at the boy.

Reggie crouched down next to Eunice, prepared to spread her towel, but Eunice shot her the kind of look that, if looks could kill, would have put Reggie in the ambulance at once.

"Who does she think she is, anyway?" said Reggie feebly, and backed away.

Joy had a baby-sitting job for the next three afternoons, and Eunice didn't see her. She mooned around the house, causing her mother to ask if she felt all right.

"She looks lovesick to me," said Millie.

Eunice, staring out the window at the plum tree, did not deign to reply.

"The first time I fell in love was the summer after sixth grade," said Millie, coming to stand beside her. "Paul Rinaldo. He had eyes like plums dipped in water, I swear. People who call it puppy love—they're either pathetic dullards or just don't remember. I'd have mugged my best friend if it would've made Paul Rinaldo like me, I swear."

"Spare me," said Eunice, but Millie wasn't listening. She stared out the window, her face rapt.

45

"Four years later and I still sometimes think of him. His father got transferred to New Mexico. I cried myself to sleep for a month, I swear."

"Bring on the violins."

Eunice ran up to her room. She pulled out a scrapbook she'd been saving and began pasting in mementos of things she and Joy had done together. Right on the front page she pasted the ancient photo of the two of them with their arms thrown around each other's shoulders, grinning without any front teeth.

She was working on it early the next afternoon when a pebble pinged off her screen. Looking down, she saw Joy on her ten-speed, a towel around her neck.

"You're here already? I didn't even eat lunch yet."

Joy dismissed this remark with a wave of her hand. "It's too hot to eat."

Lack of appetite—wasn't that one of those sure signs of love? Eunice, feeling a little queasy herself, held the scrapbook up to the window.

"I have something to show you!"

"Later, Eu! Come on!"

Eunice, with a growing sense of dread, went down. Joy was wearing a new wispy white blouse over a new hot-pink suit. As Eunice stared she blushed and gave a nervous laugh.

"It's my reward for spending three days taking

care of those Musselman brats," she said, and then asked, "Do you think it looks okay?"

Seeing Joy self-conscious made Eunice feel very eerie. But not nearly as eerie as realizing that Joy had breasts. Breasts! Had she grown them in three days? Or had they been there for a while now, just not so noticeable in her old bleached-out suit?

"It looks . . . you know it looks great, Joy."

Joy's anxious expression vanished. "It's the first time I've gone shopping without you in a million years. I needed the Eunice Gottlieb Seal of Approval!"

As they rode to the pool Eunice told herself it was ridiculous to feel betrayed by two strategically placed bulges. Gliding no-handed down Cedar Hill, she tried to remember the time when she and Joy had bragged about how many days it had been since they'd had a bath. But it was like trying to recall how they'd ever been so disgusting as to wad up their cupcake papers and chew them. One look at Joy in her new suit and she knew those days were gone forever.

At the pool they showed their passes and went into the locker room, which smelled as usual like wet paper towels and hundred-year-old tennis shoes. Stepping across the cement floor, which was pocked with grimy puddles, Eunice said loudly, "God. This place is so revolting."

"Huh? What are you so grumpy about?" Joy had

already slipped out of her shorts and blouse and tossed them into the locker they shared.

"I'm not grumpy. I just wonder sometimes if swimming here is worth the risk of contracting typhoid fever. Or," she added, making her voice meaningful, "worse."

She knew Joy knew what she meant. But Joy only made her don't-be-a-nerd grimace and, using the open locker door as a barre, began to do a series of dance warm-ups.

"I never liked coming here," Eunice went on, tugging off her own clothes, "even when we were little. Hey, remember swimming lessons? The only good part was free swim. We'd always be 'buddies.' Remember the time . . ."

Joy nodded impatiently and glanced toward the door. Eunice, her heart sinking, tried one more tactic to delay their going out to the pool.

"I have to go to the bathroom," she said.

"Okay," said Joy, slinging her dazzlingly white towel around her neck. "Meet you outside." And away she danced.

Eunice sat down on the bench. Her own towel slipped into a puddle, and she watched one corner soak up athlete's foot. She could just put her clothes on and ride home. Imagine Joy's surprise when she found her best friend gone! Found herself *alone*. Joy could talk all she wanted about how she didn't care about "fitting in," but when it came right down to it even she would have to admit there was nothing scarier or lonelier than being the odd one out. Joy could be thoughtless, but as her best friend, Eunice owed it to her not to abandon her.

Eunice picked up her pencil and crossword book. Clutching her disease-ridden towel to her nonexistent chest, she marched out the door just in time to see the dark-eyed, tangle-haired boy speak to Joy for the first time. Joy froze, there on the ladder, like someone in a fairy tale tapped by a magic wand. And then, as Eunice watched, Joy answered him.

Did a cloud really pass across the sun?

"I don't know why I bother to come to this yucky pool at all," whined Reggie Ackeroyd in Eunice's ear. "Considering I have my own Olympic-sized pool in my own backyard."

The boy stood up, and he and Joy walked over to a bench together. His friends yelled something, but he ignored them. Joy bent her head and regarded one slender, extended foot as the boy sat down. Looking up into Joy's face, he went on talking to her.

Eunice stumbled, collapsing onto her towel.

"It's kidney-shaped," said Reggie, and sat right down beside her.

That was how it went. Nearly every afternoon

Joy would call for Eunice, they would ride to the pool together, and the boy would claim her. His name was Robert Moffett and he was going to be in eighth grade. He lived on the other side of Fairmount, he played soccer, and last year he had been vice president of his class. Joy related all this to Eunice exactly as she had every detail of her life: as if Eunice had a right to know and as if, of course, Eunice would be interested.

"He likes me," she said, staring up into the plum tree, where the fruit was plump and ripening. "The first time he saw me there on the diving board, he decided he wanted to get to know me."

Eunice swallowed. "You mean he . . . he actually came right out and told you that?"

Joy laughed in a way Eunice had never heard before. "Uh huh. You could tell it never entered his cement head that I might not like him back. Not *Robert Moffett.*" She laughed again.

Eunice felt a flicker of hope. Pulling a leaf off the tree she said, "He's so handsome. I mean, it's almost unnatural." She studied Joy's upturned face, but Joy only gave that laugh again. *Flirty,* that's what it is, Eunice realized with horror. She rushed on, "The first time I saw him I thought, 'Anyone that handsome can't be capable of scratching his head and crossing the street at the same time.' And now you tell me he's not only dumb but conceited, too. What a shame."

Joy blinked, and turned to look at Eunice as if through a fog. "I didn't say that."

"Yes, you did."

"No, I didn't. I said ... oh, I can't remember what I said." She stood up slowly, yawning. "Lately I feel so ... so sleepy!" She laughed one more time and climbed onto her bike. Eunice watched her go wobbling down the driveway as if, indeed, in a trance.

Joy began wearing mascara—waterproof, of course. Once they got to the pool she did one token dive and then sat with Robert Moffett and his cohort. For a few days Eunice, at Joy's urging, sat with them too. Nobody talked to her, but nobody made fun of her, either. She could see that Robert Moffett was too big a big shot for anyone to bother his girlfriend's friend.

Then one day some of them began teasing a short redheaded boy whose voice, they said, was exactly like Woody Woodpecker's. This boy jumped up and rat-tailed his towel at Robert Moffett. Robert and another boy grabbed his arms and legs and started hauling him toward the pool. The girls shrieked; the lifeguard blew her whistle; they dropped the boy in an ignominious heap. Joy smiled and Eunice, watching Woody Woodpecker attempt to pick himself up with dignity, thought she would burst into tears.

The next day she told Joy she guessed she'd rather sit alone.

"Why?"

"I don't fit in."

"Come on, Eu! You don't even try! You never say a word!"

"They're too smooth for me."

"You don't even know them! You're just judging them on the surface!"

"Of course I am!" exploded Eunice. "That's how they judge everyone else! Why shouldn't I judge them the same way?"

Joy turned the key in the locker she and Eunice shared every day. "You don't know them," she said again, quietly.

"I don't want to."

"Okay." She handed Eunice the key. "It's up to you."

Still, day after day, Eunice went to the pool and lay doing her crossword puzzles. She wasn't sure why, when Joy came pinging a pebble on her screen every afternoon, she didn't just dump a bucket of water down on her head. Sometimes she told herself it was so that when Joy finally woke up and realized what creeps Robert and his gang were, she could turn and find her steadfast old friend waiting. Other times, usually late at night as she lay awake thinking of junior high (the Back-to-School ads had started, giving her acute heebie-jeebies), she thought it was to fool herself into feeling she and Joy still had some connection. As long as she was there, baking in plain view on the concrete, Joy couldn't forget her completely.

"A three-letter word for 'vital juice,'" she said aloud.

"Sap," said Reggie Ackeroyd in her mosquito voice.

Reggie's paper-white skin was peeling from her nose to her toes. She wore a two-piece bright orange suit that even someone with Eunice's limited fashion sense could tell was a grievous mistake. But Reggie wasn't as dumb as she appeared. Between the two of them—Eunice chewing on her pencil, Reggie yanking on her ponytail—they solved puzzle after puzzle.

"Someday maybe you can come swim in my pool," Reggie said. "You should see it. It's beautiful. Everybody who sees it says it's the most beautiful pool they've ever seen."

She looked at Eunice with an eagerness that made Eunice wince.

And then one afternoon, when Eunice was expecting Joy to show up any minute, the phone rang.

"Eu? I'm not going swimming today."

"Oh?" Eunice, standing in the kitchen, gripped the edge of the sink. Joy and Robert had had a fight. It was over. There were still two weeks before school started, plenty of time to make up, become best friends again, and behave as if Robert

Moffett had been the purest figment of the imagination. . . . "You're not?"

"No. Robert . . . Robert's taking me to the movies."

"Oh." Eunice focused on a bloated tea bag lying in the sink drain. "The movies."

"Yeah. We're going to see *Call of the Wild* at World East. It's supposed to be excellent." Joy paused. "Eu? Are you there?"

Eunice stared at the discarded tea bag. "World East? Better bring a sweater. The air-conditioning's arctic in there." She swallowed. "Unhealthy."

She could hear Joy draw a breath. She could *see* Joy's amber-colored eyebrows rush together the way they did before she began to speak carefully. Realizing how well she knew her friend made her eyes burn, and she gripped the sink all the harder.

"Eu, you're making too big a deal out of this. Just because we're going to the movies . . ."

"I just don't want you to catch cold," Eunice interrupted, and even as she tried to stop herself something made her blunder on. "Of course you probably won't need a sweater after all. Just being with the mighty Robert Moffett will probably keep you plenty warm."

There was a silence in which Eunice, the blood pounding in her ears, didn't even try to imagine what Joy looked like.

"I'm sorry you're taking this this way," said Joy.

"What way?"

"Really sorry." And Joy hung up.

Eunice banged the receiver back in its cradle. She was already in her swimming suit, and without giving herself time to think she jumped on her bike and rode to the pool. As soon as she spread her towel, Reggie Ackeroyd materialized.

"You came by yourself," she said.

"You're so observant, Reggie. Have you ever considered a career as a private eye?" Eunice, to her horror, felt the back of her throat close up and her eyes fill with tears. She turned away. Wouldn't that just top it all off? To have a jerk like Reggie see her cry?

Reggie was quiet for a moment, then said, for the seventeen-thousandth time, "I don't know why I come to this yucky pool."

"Neither do I!" Eunice burst out, turning on her. "Neither do I! Why don't you just stay home and swim in your own pool, if it's so goddamn great?"

Reggie tugged on her ponytail so hard Eunice could see her temples turn pink. She would, just then, have gladly yanked the fool thing clean off Reggie's head.

"You don't have to take it out on me," said Reggie, her lower lip trembling. "Just because your best friend dumped you . . ."

"Are you totally crazy or what? Have you completely lost your marbles? Huh? Have you?"

"I know. I saw." Reggie was trying to gather up

her stuff, fumbling and dropping everything. She picked up the crossword book by mistake, and Eunice snatched it back.

We're not pieces of a puzzle, Joy had said, light-years ago. *We're individuals.* What a liar! She'd snatched the first chance she got to fit in, and Eunice could just go rot.

"I don't blame you for being jealous," snuffled Reggie, folding up her designer towel. "I'd be jealous, too. But you don't have to . . ."

"Look, Reggie, let me give you some advice. There are times when you should just keep your mouth shut, understand?"

Reggie looked at her with pink eyes and red eyelids. "Want to come swim in my pool?"

Losers. It really did take one to know one.

"Sure. Fine. I'll come swim in your famous pool. What do I care?"

It was a long ride back to Reggie's house, one of the Tudor-style near-mansions on Fairmount Boulevard. With every push of her pedals Eunice pushed back her thoughts. She couldn't stand to think of what she and Joy had said to each other. At Reggie's they dropped their bikes on the spectacularly green grass and walked around to the back. Lying there still and empty, reflecting the sky and the late summer flowers that surrounded it, the pool was as beautiful as Reggie had claimed.

"Go on," said Reggie happily. "Go on in. It's not cold."

Eunice sat on the pool's edge and dangled her feet in the water. It was so quiet here—no shouting and splashing. She could actually hear a bird singing. The water smelled like water, not chemicals. Why, after all, did Reggie go to that foul town pool when she could have all this to herself?

Because no one wants to be alone. And Eunice felt the pain that had been building up come breaking over her.

Just then there was a familiar sound, and Eunice looked up to see Reggie bouncing on the end of the board. God! What was wrong with that girl? All knees and elbows—she'd no doubt do a belly-whopper, incur a concussion . . .

But Reggie, with one more bounce, rose, cut down through the air like a sharp little knife, and sliced into the water.

For one moment she had been nearly as graceful as Joy.

She surfaced and, treading water, smiled shyly at Eunice.

"I didn't know you could dive like that."

"I told you I had private lessons."

"I know, but you never dive at the town pool."

"Yeah. I can't do it there. Only here, in my own pool." She hoisted herself out of the water and threw herself face down on a chaise lounge.

Eunice looked down into the water and saw her own ripply reflection. It was just how she felt—watery, wavery, all her edges gone liquid.

She let herself think of Joy, who right this very moment might be having her shoulder encircled by the stupid honey-tan arm of Robert Moffett. Just the way Eunice had encircled it, in that photo where they were both front-toothless. There was no escaping the fact: no matter what turned out with Robert Moffett, things would never be the same between her and Joy again. Joy, never a cowerer, had broken the old bond. She'd meant it when she said she was sorry—Eunice knew her well enough to know she'd truly meant it. But she'd done it anyway. She wanted to be friends with Eunice, but she wanted Robert too.

A little breeze wrinkled her reflection again, and a small yellow leaf came sailing by. Autumn. Seventh grade. So this was how it was. Inside everyone was a part that yearned to be liked and to fit in, and a part that was whole all by itself.

It was going to be a rough year.

"Do you want some lemonade?" shrilled Reggie. "Or a Coke?"

Eunice knew—she'd heard in that voice she knew so well—that Joy still wanted to be friends. Now it was up to Eunice.

"Or Seven-Up?" begged Reggie.

Eunice turned to look at her. "You really can

dive," she said. Reggie's face swallowed itself up with delight at the first kind words Eunice had ever spoken to her.

"Or how about ice cream sodas? We have a machine that makes seltzer water. It's from France. We can have whatever we want, you know."

"Oh yeah?"

Eunice turned back to the pool. She looked down into the water, and saw her reflection slowly smooth itself out and stare back up at her.

On Shark's Tooth Beach

by E. L. Konigsburg

When someone challenges you on your own ground, you can't help wanting to win. And the more you want it, the harder you try. But how much does victory cost?

My dad is Hixon of Hixon's landing, the fishing camp down on the intracoastal waterway just across Highway A1A. Our camp isn't a fancy one. Just two coolers, one for beer and one for bait, plus four boats and eight motors that we rent out.

Dad was raised on a farm in Nebraska, but he joined the Navy and signed on for the war in Vietnam and came back knowing two things. One, he hated war, and two, he loved the sea. Actually, he came back with two loves. The other one was my mother. There wasn't any way anyone could get him to settle anywhere that was far from the ocean when he got out of the service, so he bought this small stretch of land in north Florida, and we've been there for all of my life that I can remember.

Dad's got this small pension for getting wounded over in Nam, so between what we sell, what we rent and what the government sends, we do all right. We're not what you're likely to call rich, but we are all right. Mom doubts that we'll ever make enough money to pay for a trip to her native country of Thailand, but she doesn't seem to mind. She says that it is more important to love where you're at than to love where you're from.

Mom makes and sells sandwiches for the fishermen. She does a right good job on them, I can tell you. There is this about Mom's sandwiches: you don't have to eat halfway through to the middle to find out what's between the bread, and once you get hold of a bite, you don't have to guess at whether it is egg salad or tuna that you're eating. The filling is high in size and in flavor.

The town next door to us is spreading south toward our landing, and both Mom and Dad say that our property will be worth a pretty penny in a few years. But both of them always ask, "What's a pretty penny worth when you can't buy anything prettier than what you already have?" I have to agree. Maybe because I don't know anything else, but I can't imagine what it would be like not to have a sandbox miles and miles long and a pool as big as an ocean for a playground across the street—even if the street is a highway. I can't ever remember going to sleep but that I heard some water shushing and slurping or humming and hollering for a lullaby.

Last spring, just as the days were getting long enough that a person could both start and finish something between the time he got home from school and the time he went to bed, I went out onto our dock and I saw this guy all duded up from a catalogue. Now that the town has grown toward us, we have more of these guys than we used to. When you've been in the business of fishing all your life, you come to know the difference between fishermen and guys who have a hobby. Here are some of the clues:

1. The hat. A real fisherman's hat is darkened

along the edges where the sweat from his hand leaves marks. A non-fisherman's hat has perfect little dent marks in it.

2. The smile. Real fishermen don't smile while they're fishing unless someone tells them a joke. Real fishermen wear their faces in the same look people wear when they are in church—deliberate and far-off—the way they do when they don't want to catch the eye of the preacher. The only time that look changes is when they take a swig of beer and then it changes only a little and with a slow rhythm like watching instant replay on television. Non-fishermen twitch their necks around like pigeons, which are very citified birds, and non-fishermen smile a lot.

3. The umbrella. Real fishermen don't have them.

This old guy sat on a wooden-legged, canvas-bottom folding campstool that didn't have any salt burns on it anywhere and put his rod into one of the holders that Dad had set up along the dock railing. Then he held out his hand and called out, "Hey, boy, do you know what I've got here?"

I walked on over to him and said, "Name's Ned."

"What's that?" he asked, cupping his hand over his ear so that the breeze wouldn't blow it past him.

"I said that my name is Ned," I repeated.

"All right, Ed," he said. "I have a question for you. Do you know what this is, boy?"

"Name's Ned," I repeated. I looked down at the palm of his hand and saw a medium-sized shark's tooth from a sand shark. "Not bad," I said.

"But do you know what it is, boy?" he asked.

I could tell that it wasn't the kind of question where a person is looking for an answer; it was the kind of question where a person just wants you to look interested long enough so that he can get on with telling you the answer. I decided that I wouldn't play it that way even if he was a customer. Three *boys* in a row made me mean, so I said, "Medium-sized sand."

"What's that?" he shouted, cupping his hand over his ear again.

"Medium-sized sand," I repeated louder.

"That's a shark's tooth," he said, clamping his hand shut.

Shoot! I knew that it was a shark's tooth. I was telling him what *kind* it was and what size it was.

"That is a fossilized shark's tooth, boy," he said. "Found it just across the street."

"Name's Ned," I told him, and I walked away.

Sharks' teeth wash up all the time at the beach just across the road from Hixon's Landing. There's a giant fossil bed out in the ocean somewheres, and a vent from it leads right onto our beach. When the undertow gets to digging up out of that fossil bed and the tide is coming in, all kinds of interesting things wash in. Besides the sharks' teeth, there are also pieces of bones that wash up. I collect the backbones, the vertebras, they're called; they have a hole in them where the spinal column went through. I have a whole string of them fixed according to size.

I collect sharks' teeth, too. I have been doing it for years. Mom started me doing it. It was Mom who made a study of them and found what kind of animal they might come from. Mom has these thorough ways about her. Dad says that Mom is smarter'n a briar and prettier'n a movie star.

Mom fixes the sharks' teeth that we collect into patterns and fastens them down onto a velvet mat and gets them framed into a shadowbox frame. She sells them down at the gift shop in town. And the gift shop isn't any tacky old gift shop full of smelly candles and ashtrays with the name of our town stamped on them. It's more like an art gallery. Matter of fact, it is called *The Artists' Gallery*, and Mom is something of an artist at how she makes those sharks' teeth designs. Some of the really pretty sharks' teeth Mom sells to a jeweler who sets them in gold for pendants. When she gets two pretty ones that match, he makes them into earrings.

When I find her a really special or unusual one, Mom says to me, "Looks like we got a trophy, Ned." When we get us a trophy, one that needs investigating or one that is just downright super special, we don't sell it. Shoot! We don't even think about selling it. There's nothing that bit of money could buy that we'd want more than having that there trophy.

Most everyone who comes to Hixon's Landing knows about Mom and me being something of authorities on fossils, especially sharks' teeth, so I figured that this old dude would either go away and not come back or hang around long enough to find out. Either way, I figured that I didn't need to advertise for myself and my mom.

The next day after school there was the old fellow again. I wouldn't want to sound braggy or anything, but I could tell that he was standing there at the end of our dock waiting for me to come home from school.

"Hi," I said.

"Well, boy," he said, "did you have a good day at school?"

"Fair," I answered. I decided to let the *boy* ride. I figured that he couldn't hear or couldn't remember or both. "Catch anything?" I asked.

"No, not today," he said. "Matter of fact I was just about to close up shop." Then he began reeling in, looking back over his shoulder to see if I was still hanging around. He didn't even bother taking the hook off his line; he just dumped rod and reel down on the dock and stuck out his hand to me and said, "Well, son, you can call me President Bob."

"What are you president of?" I asked.

"President of a college, upstate Michigan. But I'm retired now."

"Then you're not a president," I said.

"Not at the moment, but the title stays. The way that people still call a retired governor, *Governor*. You can call me President Bob instead of President Kennicott. Bob is more informal, but I wouldn't want you to call me just Bob. It doesn't seem respectful for a boy to call a senior citizen just Bob."

"And you can call me Ned," I said. "That's my name."

"All right, son," he said.

"After the first day, I don't answer to *son* or to *boy*," I said.

"What did you say your name was, son?"

Shoot! He had to learn. So I didn't answer.

"What is your name again?"

"Ned."

"Well, Ned, would you like to take a walk on the beach and hunt for some of those sharks' teeth?"

"Sure," I said.

He must have counted on my saying yes, because the next thing I see is him dropping his pants and showing me a pair of skinny white legs with milky blue veins sticking out from under a pair of bathing trunks.

As we walked the length of the dock, he told me that he was used to the company of young men since he had been president of a college. "Of course, the students were somewhat older," he said. Then he laughed a little, like punctuation. I didn't say anything. "And, of course, I didn't often see the students on a one-to-one basis." I didn't say anything. "I was president," he added. He glanced over at me, and I still didn't say anything. "I was president," he added.

"There's supposed to be some good fishing in Michigan," I said.

"Oh, yes! Yes, there is. Good fishing. Fine fishing. Sportsmen's fishing."

We crossed A1A and got down onto the beach from a path people had worn between the dunes, and I showed him how to look for sharks' teeth in the coquina. "There's nothing too much to learn," I said. "It's mostly training your eye."

He did what most beginners do, that is, he picked up a lot of wedge-shaped pieces of broken shell, mostly black, thinking they were fossil teeth. The tide was just starting on its way out, and that is the best time for finding sharks' teeth. He found about eight of them, and two of them were right nice sized. I found fourteen myself and three of mine were bigger than anything he collected. We compared, and I could tell that he was wishing he had mine, so I gave him one of my big ones. It wasn't a trophy or anything like that because I would never do that to Mom, that is, give away a trophy or a jewelry one.

President Bob was waiting for me the next day

and the day after that one. By the time Friday afternoon came, President Bob gave up on trying to pretend that he was fishing. He'd just be there on the dock, waiting for me to take him shark's tooth hunting.

"There's no magic to it," I told him. "You can go without me."

"That's all right, Ned," he said, "I don't mind waiting."

On Saturday I had a notion to sleep late and was in the process of doing just that when Mom shook me out of my sleep and told me that I had a visitor. It was President Bob, and there he was standing on his vanilla legs right by my bedroom door. He had gotten tired of waiting for me on the dock. It being Saturday, he had come early so's we could have more time together.

Mom invited him in to have breakfast with me, and while we ate, she brought out our trophy boxes. Our trophies were all sitting on cotton in special boxes like the ones you see butterflies fixed in inside a science museum. Mom explained about our very special fossils.

"Oh, yes," President Bob said. Then, "Oh, yes," again. Then after he'd seen all our trophies and had drunk a second cup of coffee, he said, "We had quite a fine reference library in my college. I am referring to the college of which I was president. Not my alma mater, the college I attended as a young man. We had quite a fine library, and I must confess I used it often, so I am not entirely unfamiliar with these things."

That's when I said, "Oh, yes," except that it came out, "Oh, yeah!" and that's when Mom swiped my foot under the table.

President Bob plunked his empty cup down on the table and said, "Well, come on now, Ned, time and tide wait for no man. Ha! Ha!"

I think that I've heard someone say that at least four times a week. Everyone says it. Dad told me that it was a proverb, an old, old saying. And I can tell you that it got old even before I reached my second birthday.

When we got down to the beach, President Bob brought out a plastic bag and flung it open like a bag boy at the supermarket. But there wasn't much to fill it with that day because the currents had shifted and weren't churning up the fossil bed.

"I suppose you'll be going to church tomorrow," he said.

"Yes," I answered.

"I think I'll do some fishing in the morning. I'll probably have had enough of that by noon. I'll meet you at the dock about twelve-thirty. We can get started on our shark's tooth hunt then."

"Sorry," I said. "I help Mom with the sandwiches and then we clean things up and then we go to late services. Sunday is our busiest day."

"Of course it is," he said.

Mom and I got back about one-thirty and changed out of our good clothes before Dad came in as he always does on Sundays to grab some lunch before the men start coming back and he has to get busy with washing down motors and buying. (What he buys is fish from the men who have had a specially good run. Dad cleans them and sells them to markets back in town or to people who drive on out toward the beach of a Sunday. Sometimes, he gets so busy buying and cleaning that Mom and I pitch right in and give him a hand.)

Dad had not quite finished his sandwiches and had just lifted his beer when he got called out to the dock. There was this big haul of bass that some men were wanting to sell.

Mom and I were anxious to finish our lunch and clean up so's we could go on out and see if Dad would be needing some help when President Bob presented himself at the screen door to our kitchen.

"Knock, knock," he said, pressing his old face up against the screen. The minute we both looked up he opened the door without even an *if you please* and marched into our kitchen on his frosted icicle legs. "I think you're going to be interested in what I found today," he said. "Very interested."

Mom smiled her customer smile and said, "We are having very busy day, please to excuse if I continue with work."

"That's perfectly all right," President Bob said. "You're excused." Then he sat down at the table that Mom was wiping off. He held up the placemat and said, "Over here, Mama-san. You missed a spot."

Mom smiled her customer smile again and wiped the spot that he had pointed to, and President Bob put the placemat back down and emptied the contents of his plastic bag right on top of it. He leaned over the pile and using his forefinger began to comb through it. "Ah! here," he said. He picked up a small black thing between his thumb and forefinger and said to Mom, "Come here, Mama-san." *Mama-san* is some kind of Japanese for *mama*. A lot of people call my mom that, but she says it's okay because it is a term of respect, and a lot of people think that all Orientals are Japanese. Sometimes these same people call me Boy-san, which is to *boy* what Mama-san is to mama. They call me that because I have dark slanted eyes just like Mom's, except that hers are prettier.

"Look at this," President Bob said. "Look at it closely. I suspect that it is the upper palate of an extinct species of deep-water fish."

Mom took it from his hand and looked at it and said, "Dolphin tooth." She put it back down and walked to the sink where she continued right on with washing up the dishes. She automatically handed me a towel to dry.

President Bob studied the dolphin's tooth and said to Mom, "Are you sure?"

She smiled and nodded.

"Quite sure?"

She nodded.

He asked once more, and she nodded again. Then he began poking through his collection again and came up with another piece. He beckoned to Mom to look at it closer, and she dried her hands and did that.

"Shell," she said.

"Oh, I beg to differ with you," he said.

"Shell," Mom said, looking down at it, not bothering to pick it up.

"Are you sure?"

She nodded.

"Quite sure?"

She nodded again, and I came over and picked it up off the table and held it up and broke it in two. I thought that President Bob was going to arrest me. "A piece of fossil that thick wouldn't break that easy. It's a sure test," I said.

"There are fragile fossils, I'm sure," President Bob said.

"I suppose so," I said. "But that shell ain't fossilized. Piece of fossil that thick wouldn't ever break that easy." I could see that you had to repeat yourself with President Bob. "That shell ain't fossilized."

"*Ain't* is considered very bad manners up North," President Bob said.

Shoot! *Bad manners* are considered bad manners down South, I thought. But I didn't say anything. President Bob kept sorting through his bag of stuff, studying on it so hard that his eyes winched up and made his bottom jaw drop open.

Mom finished washing the dishes, and I finished drying, and we asked if we could be excused, and President Bob told us (in our own kitchen, mind) that it was perfectly all right, but would we please fetch him a glass of ice water before we left. We fetched it. He said, "Thank you. You may go now." I suppose that up North it's good manners to give people orders in their own house if you do it with *please* and *thank you* and no *ain't*s.

It rained on Monday and it rained again on Tuesday, so I didn't see President Bob again until Wednesday after school. He was waiting for me at the end of the dock with his plastic sandwich bag already partly full. "Well," he said, "I guess I got a bit of a head start on you today."

I looked close at his bag and saw that he had a couple of nice ones—not trophies, but nice.

"I have homework," I said. "I can't walk the beaches with you today."

"What subject?"

"Math."

"Maybe I can help you. Did I tell you that I was president of a college?"

"Really?" I said in my fakiest voice. "I think I better do my homework by myself."

"I'll wait for you," he said. "I promise I won't hunt for anything until you come back out."

"It'll probably take me the rest of daylight to do it," I said.

"Math must be hard for you," he said. "Always was my strongest subject."

"It's not hard for me," I lied. "I just have a lot of it."

"Let me show you what I found today," he said.

"I don't think I have the time."

"Just take a minute."

Before I could give him another polite no, he had spread the contents of his bag over the railing of the dock. I looked things over real good. I knew he was watching me, so I wouldn't let my eyes pause too long on any one thing in particular. "Very nice," I said. "I've got to go now."

As I turned to walk back to our house, he called, "See you tomorrow."

The next day I didn't even walk to the dock. Instead I walked around to the side door of our house and threw my books on the wicker sofa on the screened porch and went up to my room and changed into my cut-offs. I had a plan; I was going to go back out the side door and walk a bit to the north before crossing the highway and climbing over the dunes onto the beach. I knew a place where a sandbar often formed, and Mom and I sometimes went there. When I was little, she'd put me in the sloop behind the sandbar, like at a wading pool at a regular Holiday Inn. As I got older, we'd go there on lazy days and take a picnic lunch and sift through the coquina of the sandbar. We've found about four trophies there. Not about, exactly four. Of the four, the first one was the most fun because it was the one we found by accident.

I felt if I could get out of the house and head north, I could escape President Bob and dig up some trophies that would make him flip.

But I didn't escape. When I came downstairs after changing my clothes, there he was sitting on the wicker sofa, his blueberry ripple legs crossed in front of him. He was leafing through my math book.

I told him hello.

He smiled at me. "Yes, yes, yes," he said, "I know exactly how it is to have to sit in school all day and have to hold your water. I am quite used to the habits of young men. I was president of a liberal arts college in Michigan." He noticed that I was wearing my cut-offs, my usual beachcombing outfit, so he slapped his thighs and set them to shimmying like two pots of vanilla yogurt. "I see you're ready. Let's get going. The tide's halfway out already, and as they say, 'Time and tide wait for no man.' Tide was better a few hours ago. I found a couple of real beauties. Locked them in the glove compartment of my car."

I walked with him to the beach, and we began our hunt. He wasn't bending over for falsies very much anymore. Each time he bent over, he yelled, "Got one!" and then he'd hold it up in the air and wouldn't put it in his bag until I nodded or said something or both. President Bob ended up with about twenty teeth and one vertebra bone, and of the twenty, one was a real trophy, an inch long, heavy root and the whole edge serrated with nothing worn away. A real trophy.

I found eight. Three of them were medium, four of them were itty-bitty and one had the tip crushed off.

I got up early the next day and checked the tide; it was just starting out. Good, I thought. I crossed the road and ran out onto the beach, rolling up my pajama bottoms as I walked along. The tide was just right; it was leaving long sawtooth edges of coquina, and I managed to collect eight decent-sized teeth and one right-good-sized one before I ran back home and hosed off my feet and got dressed for school. I stuffed my collection into the pockets of my cut-offs. I had to skip breakfast, a fact that didn't particularly annoy me until about eleven o'clock. That afternoon, for every two times President Bob stooped down and yelled, "Got one!" I did it three times.

On Friday I didn't want to skip breakfast again, and my mother for sure didn't want me to, so President Bob was way ahead.

On Saturday I got up before dawn and dressed and sat on our dock until I saw the first thin line of dawn. Dawn coming over the intracoastal is like watching someone draw up a venetian blind. On a clear day the sky lifts slowly and evenly, and it makes a guy feel more than okay to see it happen. But on that Saturday, I sat on the dock just long enough to make sure that daylight was to the east of me before I crossed the highway and began heading north. Shoot! I think that if the Lord had done some skywriting that morning, I wouldn't have taken the time to read it, even if it was in English.

Finally, I climbed to the top of a tall dune and walked up one and down another. I was heading for a place between the dunes about a mile to the north. I knew that during spring, when the moon was new, there was a tidewater between two of the dunes. Sharks' teeth got trapped in it, and sometimes Mom and I would go there if there was a special size she was looking for to finish an arrangement. You had to dig down into the coquina, and it wasn't much fun finding sharks' teeth this way instead of sauntering along the beach and happening to find them. But sometimes it was necessary.

I dug.

I dug and I dug and I dug.

I put all my findings into a clam shell that I found, and I dug, and I dug, and I dug. I felt the sun hot on my back, and I still dug. I had my back to the ocean and my face to the ground and for all I knew there was no sky and no sea and no sand and no colors. There was nothing, nothing and nothing except black, and that black was the black of fossil teeth.

I had filled the clam shell before I stopped digging. I sorted the teeth and put the best ones—there were fourteen of them—in my right side pocket—the one with a button—and I put all the smaller ones in my back pocket and started back toward home, walking along the strand. I figured that I had a good head start on the day and on President Bob. I would pepper my regular findings with the ones I had just dug up. I'd mix the little ones in with the fourteen big ones. But, I decided, smiling to myself, I'd have a run of about eight big ones in a row just to see what he would do.

My back felt that it was near to burning up, and I looked toward the ocean, and it looked powerful good. The morning ocean in the spring can be as blue as the phony color they paint it on a geography book map. Sometimes there are dark patches in it, and the gulls sweep down on top of the dark spots. I decided that I needed to take a dip in that ocean. I half expected a cloud of steam to rise up off my back. I forgot about time and tide and sharks' teeth and ducked under the waves and licked the salt off my lips as I came back up.

I was feeling pretty good, ready to face President Bob and the world, and then I checked my pockets and found that half the supply from my back pocket had tumbled out, and I had lost two big ones. I was pretty upset about that, so I slowed down on my walk back home. I crouched down and picked up shell pieces, something I thought that I had outgrown, but that is about how anxious I was not to let anything get by me. I found a couple of medium-sized ones and put them in my back pocket and began a more normal walk when my trained eye saw a small tooth right at the tide line.

I reached down to pick it up, figuring that, if nothing else, it would add bulk to my collection the way they add cereal to hot dog meat. I didn't have any idea how many baby teeth I had lost out of my back pocket.

When I reached down to pick up that little tooth, it didn't come up immediately, and I began to think that maybe it was the tip of a really big one. I stooped down and carefully scraped away the wet sand and saw that there were several teeth together. The tide was rushing back up to where I was, so I laid my hand flat down on the ground and shoveled up a whole fistful of wet, cool sand.

I walked back to the dune and gently scraped away the sand with the forefinger of my other hand, and then I saw what I had.

There were several teeth, and they were attached to a piece of bone, a piece of jawbone. There was a space between the third tooth and the fourth, and the smallest tooth, the one on the end that I had first seen, was attached to the jawbone by only a thin edge.

I had never seen such a trophy. I felt that the spirit of the Lord had come mightily upon me, like Samson. Except that I had the jawbone of a shark and not the jawbone of an ass. And I wanted to smite only one president, not a thousand Philistines.

I didn't run the rest of the way home. I was too careful for that. I walked, holding that trophy in my hand, making certain that it didn't dry out before I could see if the weak tooth was fossilized onto the bone.

I called to Mom when I came into the house and when she appeared at the door to the screened porch, I uncurled my fingers one by one until the whole bone and all four of the teeth were showing. I watched Mom's face, and it was like watching the dawn I had missed.

"Ah, Ned," she said, "it is the Nobel Prize of trophies." We walked into the kitchen. She wet a good wad of paper towels and lifted the jawbone carefully from my hand and put it down on that pad of paper. And then we sat down at the kitchen table and I told her about how I found it, and I told it all to her in detail. Dad came in and Mom asked me to tell him, and I did and she listened just as hard the second time.

We ate our breakfast, and afterwards we wet

the paper towels again and moved the trophy onto a plastic placemat on the kitchen table. Mom looked at it through the magnifying glass and then handed me the glass so that I could look at it, too.

While we were studying it hard like that, President Bob came to the screen door and said, "Knock, knock."

Mom nodded at me, her way of letting me know that I was supposed to invite him on in.

"Well, well," he said. "Are we ready for today's treasure hunt?"

"I guess so," I said, as easy as you please, moving a little to the left so that he could catch a glimpse of what Mom and I were looking at.

He gave it a glance and then another one right quick.

Mom and I looked at each other as he came closer and closer to the table. He studied that trophy from his full height and from behind a chair. Next thing, he moved in front of the chair. And next after that he sat down in the chair. And then, not taking his eyes off that trophy, he held his hand out for the magnifying glass and Mom took it from me and gave it to him.

The whole time he did this, I watched his face. His eyes squinched up and his jaw dropped open and his nostrils flared. It was like watching a mini-movie called *Jealousy and Greed.*

I could feel myself smiling. "Found it this morning," I said.

Then I didn't say anything anymore. And I stopped smiling.

I thought about his face, and that made me think about mine. If his face was a movie called *Jealousy and Greed,* I didn't like the words I could put to mine.

I gently pushed the placemat closer to President Bob. "Look at it," I said. "Look at it good." I waited until his eyes were level with mine. "It's for you," I said. "It's a present from me."

"Why, thank you, boy," he said.

"Name's Ned," I answered, as I walked around to the other side of the table and emptied my pockets. "Do you think we can make something pretty out of these?" I asked Mom.

She gave me a Nobel Prize of a smile for an answer. President Bob didn't even notice, he was so busy examining the jawbone with which he had been smitten.

Splendor

by Lois Lowry

Can a new dress make all the difference? Can a very special new dress work magic?

If you answered either "Yes" or "No," you might be surprised....

THE DRESS WAS IN THE WINDOW OF A STORE CALLED Chrysalis, on a side street just off Main. It was red—but not an ordinary red; it was the bright, blinding red of nail polish, poinsettias, cinnamon hearts, and neon lights. The material glistened and shimmered, even in the gray light of the late December afternoon and through the dirt-streaked windows of the ignominious shop.

On display, the dress fell in soft folds around the rigid body of the blank-eyed mannequin; but in real life, Becky knew, on a real person (on me; she shivered, allowing herself to think it), it would almost come alive—it would move and swoop and swish. She stared, so close to the window that her breath in the bitter winter air fogged a circle on the glass. She wiped it clear with a mittened hand and breathed another awed and steamy circle in its place.

There were stars on the skirt. Hundreds of them: tiny, gold-sequined stars, an entire galaxy sewn into the brilliant crimson cloth. Above the firmament of the skirt, the bodice hugged the pointy-breasted dummy torso, the low neck draped itself around the unyielding shoulders, and the voluminous sleeves fell against the awkwardly posed putty-colored arms like petals clinging to lifeless stems.

Becky stamped her boots in the slush to warm her feet. She shifted her schoolbooks in her arms.

It was late, and she knew she should be hurrying home. But she couldn't make herself turn away. She studied the sign on the store: Chrysalis. Becky didn't know what "chrysalis" meant. But she knew what the dress meant: it meant everything. It meant beauty; music; happiness; grace and glory and glittering change. The right word came suddenly to Becky's mind, and she whispered it half aloud, still staring at the mannequin frozen in her vacant-eyed pose.

"Splendor," Becky whispered.

When she entered the shop, a tiny bell on the rim of the door tinkled. The salesgirl, perched on a stool behind the counter, engrossed in a paperback book, glanced up.

"Hi," she said, and attached her finger to a spot on the page, to mark her place.

"How much is that red dress?" Becky asked, pointing to the window.

"Thirty-nine ninety-five," said the clerk. "Made in India. It's not washable." She looked back down at her book.

Becky examined her boots and nudged some dirty snow from one with the toe of the other. "Well," she said finally, "do you have it in my size?"

The salesgirl sighed, closed her book reluctantly after bending a corner of the page, and peered skeptically over the counter at Becky. "Small, medium, large is the way it comes," she said. "But even the small would be too big for you."

"I'm tall for thirteen," Becky said, though she felt smaller than ever, as if the girl's bored gaze had caused her to shrink and dwindle inside her parka.

The salesgirl shrugged. "You can try it on if you want. Over there." She nodded her head to indicate a place across the room.

Becky looked. The fitting room was simply a corner of the store, a place where a brass-ringed curtain could be pulled across a diagonal rod to form a private triangle. It wasn't private enough, she thought. When she tried on the magnificent dress, she wanted to twirl and pose. She didn't want the smirking salesgirl to watch.

"I'll come back," she said. "Maybe tomorrow."

"Sure," said the girl, exploring her mouth with her tongue, as if a piece of lunch were caught between her teeth. She looked down and opened her book again. "You do that," she said, her eyes already on the page.

"Mom," said Becky at dinner, "I found a dress that I want for the Christmas dance. It's at this little store with a funny name, something like 'chrysanthemum,' or 'Christmas'—"

"It's 'Chrysalis,' " her sister, Angela, said, reaching for another helping of macaroni and cheese.

"Don't you even know the word *chrysalis*? You must have had it in science."

"Well, I forget," Becky said. "I don't remember every single thing I ever learned, the way you do."

"A chrysalis," Angela explained in the bored voice of a teacher going through something for the fifteenth time, "is what a caterpillar forms around itself while it goes through the changes to become a butterfly."

"That ugly gray thing? That's called a cocoon," Becky pointed out.

Angela sighed impatiently. She was only a year older than Becky, but sometimes it seemed as though they were generations apart. "Cocoon is the more common word for it," she said. "But a store can't call itself 'Cocoon,' for heaven's sake. 'Chrysalis' sounds better, and it's more scientific. I think it comes from the Greek."

" 'I think it comes from the Greek,' " mimicked Becky.

Angela ignored her. "The store's over on Harrington Street, Mom," she said. "They sell cheap imported stuff."

"It isn't cheap," Becky said defensively. "This dress costs a lot."

"Mine only cost ten dollars," Angela said smugly.

"Well, you *made* yours. Not all of us can sew," muttered Becky. Or sing, she thought, or cook, or play the piano, or get all A's in school. Angrily she listed her sister's accomplishments in her mind. "Not all of us are perfect."

"Hey," their mother said, laughing. "I don't want to listen to you two arguing. I want to hear about the *dress*."

"It costs thirty-nine ninety-five," Becky announced hesitantly.

Angela pretended to choke on her mouthful of macaroni.

But to Becky's surprise, her mother smiled. "You have your baby-sitting money in the bank, Beck," she said. "And it's your very first real dance. If you want to spend that much on a special dress—well, it's up to you."

"Mom," said Angela, "nobody dances with seventh graders anyway. The seventh-grade boys won't dance. They all stand around in the corners with each other. And the eighth-grade boys only dance with the eighth-grade girls. So what's the point of spending all your money on a dress if no one's going to dance with you? I *told* Becky she could wear my blue dress to the dance. The one I wore last year."

"I don't want to wear a hand-me-down dress, not to the Christmas dance," Becky exploded. "You didn't have to wear someone else's dress when you were in seventh grade!"

"Becky," Angela pointed out in her logical, patronizing way, "*I* didn't have an older sister. So who could hand a dress down?"

"It's not my fault I was born second."

"Shhh," said their mother. "Calm down. You buy the dress, honey, if it's what you want. It's important to have a very special dress now and then."

Becky glanced at her mother with a mixture of gratitude and, suddenly, guilt. How long had it been since her mother had had a new dress? The sweater and skirt she was wearing were ones she had had for years. Still, her mother was smiling at her. Her mother understood.

"I don't know why they let seventh graders come anyway," Angela grumbled. "Most of them are such babies."

Wait till you see me in my new dress, thought Becky as she ate her macaroni. I won't look like a baby then.

And the next night, alone in her room, gasping with delight at her own image in the mirror, she had the same thought: I don't look like a baby now.

She hadn't tried the dress on in the store; why bother, when size small was the only choice? Now, wearing it, she realized that it was, as the clerk had predicted, a little too large. But it didn't matter. The dress shimmered and swirled, as she had known it would. The petal-like sleeves engulfed her thin arms, and the neckline—the whole top, in fact—was very loose; she would have to make it tighter somehow. But the stars on the skirt sparkled as she turned in circles around her small bedroom, and the bright red glowed like flame against the pastel walls and rug.

She could picture herself three nights from now at the dance, the school gym transformed by dim lights and festive decorations into a place of magical romance, and herself transformed by the dress from a skinny seventh grader to a graceful, glamorous, changed person. It was true, what Angela had said, that the boys in her class wouldn't dance; they would stand in the corners, making jokes. But it didn't matter. Someone new would be there. Someone older. Someone who would notice her for the first time.

Becky opened her bedroom door and called, "Ready?"

"Ready!" her mother replied from the living room, and Angela began to sing loudly: "A pretty girl is like a melodeeee . . ." Becky emerged, tiptoed down the stairs, and then, walking carefully, slowly, the way she knew models did in fashion shows, she entered the room where her audience was waiting.

Angela's singing dissolved in a spasm of giggles. "It's too big!" she sputtered. "It *hangs* on you!"

Becky held her shoulders straight. "I'm going to

fix that," she said with dignity. "What do you think, Mom? Isn't it gorgeous?"

"Well," said her mother slowly, "it's certainly a very Christmassy color. Goodness, it's the reddest red I've ever seen."

"See?" said Becky gleefully to her sister. "Mom likes it!"

Angela was doubled over on the couch. She couldn't stop giggling. "It's trashy! You couldn't find a trashier-looking dress if you searched for a million years!"

Becky's shoulders slumped, and the neckline of her dress drooped. "Mom?" she asked uncertainly. "It isn't, is it?"

"It's just that it's a little sophisticated, Beck," her mother said gently. "We're not accustomed to seeing you wear something so mature. Angela, stop it."

Angela took a deep breath and sat up straight, her lips compressed against the laughter she was holding back.

"I *wanted* something sophisticated," Becky said. She felt her face getting hot, and her eyes beginning to water. "See the gold stars?" She held out the skirt with one hand, while her other hand grasped the gaping neckline to her chest. "Aren't the stars beautiful?" she asked, but her voice faltered.

"They are," her mother said. She came to Becky and hugged her. "They truly are. And we'll help you take some tucks in the top, so that it fits better. Won't we, Angela?" She gave Becky's sister a sharp look.

Angela sighed. "Sure, Beck. I'm sorry I laughed. It was just a surprise, that's all, seeing it for the first time. Now that I'm getting used to it, I can see that there are some good things about it. The material's nice and floaty."

"Yeah," said Becky, reassured. "It really swirls around."

Back upstairs, she hung the dress carefully in her closet, and looked with pleasure at the burst of color it provided there in contrast to the clothes of her ordinary life. Beside it hung an outgrown brown jumper of Angela's, and next to that Angela's old plaid skirt. It was a closet full of leftovers, Becky thought, a *life* full of leftovers—until the dress changed everything.

Happily she snuggled in her bed, still thinking of it before she went to sleep: thinking of the skirt with its cascading golden stars; anticipating the magic moment, only three nights away, when she would spin and twirl and the splendor of the dress would make her beautiful.

In the background of her fantasy, she could still hear her sister's disdainful voice. Trashy, Angela had said. But Angela had apologized; she had changed her mind. And her mother had loved the dress.

Hadn't she?

Anyway, it didn't really matter. Becky herself was the important one, and Becky knew how perfect the dress was: how dazzling the shiny red, how spectacular the fountains of bright stars on the skirt.

It was, wasn't it?

She dismissed the uncertainty, and fell asleep. But she slept fitfully, waking now and then with a feeling that she remembered having occasionally as a small child: the feeling that there might be something terrible lurking in her closet.

At school, hurrying through the hallway between Thursday's classes, someone brushed by her in the crowd and stopped. It was Heather, her sister's best friend. "Hi, Becky," Heather said. "Angela tells me you have quite a dress for the dance tomorrow night!"

Becky smiled shyly, clutching her books. "Yeah," she acknowledged. "It's red."

Heather grinned. "I heard," she said.

None of Angela's friends had ever singled Becky out before; she had always been only the little sister, the pest. Things were changing already, she realized, because of the dress. She glowed with pride, and stood up straighter, with more self-confidence. "It was a little too big," she confided in Heather, "but my mother—"

"Yeah, I heard that too," Heather said, snickering. "I understand it would look good on Bette

Midler. In fact I understand the two of you could fit into it together!"

Then she was gone, swept off by a group of laughing friends, and Becky was alone. Humiliated, she looked at the floor as she walked down the hall to her next class.

During math, as Mr. Findlay droned on and on, writing incomprehensible things on the blackboard, Becky tried to recapture her daydream, the daydream of the dress. She tried to picture herself whirling in intricate dance steps across a polished floor while a crowd watched in amazement and admiration. But try as she might, the vision was gone. All she could see was a too-gaudy, too-big, too-expensive dress; and she saw herself, not beautiful at all, but thin and awkward, out of place, and embarrassed. The paper on her desk blurred, and she put her face in her hands.

"Becky? Are you all right?" She could feel a firm touch on her shoulder. She looked up.

"I'm sorry I wasn't paying attention, Mr. Findlay," she said miserably. "I don't feel very good."

"Mom," Becky said hesitantly that evening as she helped her mother with the dishes, "I don't think I want to go to the dance."

Her mother reached up to put a plate away in the cupboard. "But you were so excited about it, honey," she said. "What's wrong?"

"Me, I guess. *I'm* wrong. At least I'm wrong for

the dress. I still love the dress, but it's too big for me, even after you took those tucks in it; and it's too old for me; and I'm afraid everyone will laugh."

Her mother dried her hands on the dish towel and smoothed Becky's dark bangs. She frowned. "Your forehead's hot, Becky. Do you feel all right?"

"No. I feel horrible."

"I think you have a fever. Why don't you go on to bed? Maybe tomorrow you'll feel better and things will look different. Don't make a decision now."

By morning there was no decision left to make. Becky's throat was sore, her head ached, and the thermometer said that her temperature was over 100 degrees. She dozed off and on all day, waking when her mother brought her aspirin and ginger ale.

At suppertime she sat up in bed and ate some soup and toast from a tray. From her room she could hear the sound of the shower, and of Angela's bureau drawers opening and closing. She pictured her sister in the next bedroom, standing in front of her mirror to fasten her tiny gold earrings, brushing her newly washed hair, smoothing the simple, pretty dress she had made. In an odd way she was happy for her sister, knowing she would be poised and popular at the dance; and she was happy for herself, that she was here in her familiar, cozy bed with a bowl of her mother's vegetable soup and a new mystery book from the library on the table beside her.

Finally she heard the doorbell downstairs, and her mother's greeting to the friends who had stopped by for Angela on their way to the dance. Becky heard her sister's footsteps starting down the stairs; then she heard them stop and turn back.

"Becky, I'm sorry you can't go," Angela said. She stood in the doorway of Becky's bedroom, her hair tied back with a ribbon that matched the soft green of her dress.

Becky smiled ruefully at her sister. "It doesn't matter," she admitted. "I don't think I really wanted to go anyway. You were right about the dress."

"It isn't actually trashy," Angela said. "I don't know why I said that. It's just a little too old for you."

Becky nodded. "And too big," she said.

"Maybe it'll fit you next year," Angela pointed out. "Remember how much I grew between seventh and eighth grades?"

"Yeah. Probably I will, too."

"And listen, Beck. At the end of the dance, they take down the decorations, and everybody gets to take something home. I'll bring you something.

There are silver stars hanging all over the ceiling of the gym. I'll see if I can get you some, okay?"

Becky smoothed the blanket over her knees and sighed. Then she grinned. "Angela," she said, "I think I've OD'd on stars. I have a closet full of them."

"Mom?" Becky called later. "Do you think I can get up? I feel better. My throat doesn't hurt at all anymore."

Her mother came to her room and assessed Becky's fever by kissing her forehead. "Okay," she decided. Then she hesitated. She stood beside Becky's bed, her head tilted as if she were thinking about something very far away. Becky watched as her mother, lost in thought, smoothed the folds of her old sweater and fingered the strand of dime-store pearls around her neck. Her mother was smiling.

"Becky," she asked, "would you do something for me? Would you put on your new dress?"

"Mom," Becky groaned, "I'm not sure I *ever* want to wear that dress!"

"Just this once, Beck. For me, okay? I have a surprise."

"There's nobody here, is there? I don't want anyone but you to see me in it."

"I promise. It's just you and me. I'll meet you in the living room in a few minutes."

"Okay," Becky said, laughing.

After her mother had gone, Becky got out of bed and took the red dress from her closet. Carefully she put it on and zipped it up. She put on stockings, and the delicate sandals she had planned to wear to the Christmas dance. She brushed her hair. Finally she stood in front of the mirror and looked at herself. The dress was still too big, and it bunched awkwardly in the places where her mother had stitched it together to try to make it fit.

But a little of the magic had returned. Suddenly, from downstairs, she could hear music; her mother had turned on the stereo. Becky turned slowly in a circle in front of the mirror, and the skirt full of stars glittered in the dim light of her bedroom. She felt giddy and light-headed—maybe from the day of fever. Or maybe it was just the feeling, once again, that she was beautiful, wearing the dress that was the reddest red any dress had ever been; and that she was safe, here, in a place where no one would laugh.

Becky started down the stairs toward the living room, where the music played softly and she could see that her mother had lighted candles. The familiar room was different now; it glowed in the unaccustomed flickering candlelight, and even the ancient, shabby furniture took on new and unfamiliar shapes as its shadows moved on the walls. The stains in the threadbare rug were blurred and muted in the softened light, and the flowered patterns of the old slipcovers were deepened into subtler shades. Everything seemed changed.

At the bottom of the stairs, Becky stopped in her tracks, and stared.

Waiting in the middle of the living room was Becky's mother, and she was wearing the most hideous dress that Becky had ever seen. It was purple: the most purple of all possible purples, a shiny satin the shade of overripe plums; and it had thin straps which were encrusted with cheap rhinestones. It was too short, well above her mother's knees. And it was too tight; a seam above the waist had begun to rip.

Her mother, who never wore makeup at all, was wearing purple eyeshadow. She had on lipstick and there were dusky smudges of rouge on her cheeks. Her hair, which was always tied back tightly at her neck, was loose, falling around her bare shoulders.

"Where did you get that dress?" Becky finally managed to gasp.

"Do you like it?" her mother asked. She held the edges of the skirt in her fingertips, and turned, posing.

"It's—" Becky said, and stopped. She had been about to say "trashy." Instead, she bit her lip and suggested, "It's a little young for you, I think."

"Of course it is." Her mother laughed. "It's also too small. You're the only person who's ever seen me wearing it."

"But, Mom, it—well, it doesn't look like you!"

"I know," her mother said, smiling. "Here; have some fake champagne. It's really ginger ale. But the champagne glasses are real crystal. I had to wash the dust off, they've been packed away so long."

Becky sipped from the fragile long-stemmed glass. She shook her head in wonder. "Where did you get it? *When* did you get it?"

Her mother sat down on the couch and smoothed the garish purple skirt. "I bought it nine years ago," she said, "and I never told a soul."

"Nine years ago?" Becky said. She calculated in her head. "I was four years old. That was the year that Daddy—"

Her mother nodded. "It was the year your father died."

Becky remembered, though she had been very small. She remembered the sense of confusion and loss, and the comfort of her mother's quiet voice. She remembered her mother holding her, rocking her in an old chair that creaked rhythmically, mournfully, endlessly, as it moved.

"I don't understand," she said to her mother.

"I'm not sure I do either, Beck," her mother confessed. "It was a few months after he died. By then everyone had stopped feeling sorry for me and paying a lot of attention to me, and all of a sudden I felt all alone—alone with two little girls, and not enough money. I felt—well, scared, I guess. And depressed. I felt as if I would never again be young, or carefree, or pretty. And then one day I walked past a store, and in the window of the store—"

"You saw that dress."

Her mother nodded, smiling, remembering. "I saw this dress. I couldn't afford it, and I certainly didn't need it. And it wasn't a beautiful dress, even then. It was a tawdry, terrible dress. But I wanted it more than I'd ever wanted anything."

"Like me. Like my dress." Becky looked down and touched her own skirt with its cheap golden stars.

"In those first couple of years, every now and then, after you girls were in bed, I would put it on. And a strange thing would happen. One part of me *knew* what an ugly dress it was. But when I put it on, something magic would happen. It made me feel younger—"

"Mine makes me feel older," Becky whispered, almost to herself.

"—and it made me feel beautiful."

"Yes," Becky breathed. "I know. Mine does, too."

"I haven't even looked at it for several years. But it's always been there, in the back of my closet. And I still, even after all this time, like to think about it now and then. I picture myself wearing it, swirling around in some imaginary ballroom ..."

"And then what?" Becky asked. "What happens?" In her own mind, silently, she was asking: Does your life change? Does everything change? Do you change?

Her mother smiled and shook her head. "Then I go and do the laundry. Or I cook dinner. I help you with your homework. Ordinary things. But I feel—well, I feel special. That's all that happens."

The record ended. Becky turned it over and started the stereo again. It was old-fashioned music, filled with violins surging in long, slow, melodic passages.

"Mom," she asked shyly, "would you dance with me?"

They danced together, moving across the living room in wide turns that made their skirts float like flowers drifting in a pond. In the dim candlelight, the purple satin glowed; and the bright red of Becky's dress was muted, softened, and warm. The sequined stars gleamed as if they were made of real gold, and the rhinestones sparkling on her mother's shoulders could have been true diamonds.

For a moment they lived in the daydream. They twirled and held each other and for a moment they were beautiful. Then they paused for breath, and collapsed together on the couch.

"I'm a terrible dancer," Becky confessed.

"Me too," her mother said. "Two left feet, that's me.

"You know what?" her mother suggested, looking first at Becky and then at herself. "Mine's too small, and yours is too big. Maybe we should trade dresses."

Becky stared at her. "But yours is so ugly!" she said. Then she looked down at herself, suddenly startled. She shook her head in amazement, and giggled. "So is mine!" she said, and laughter overwhelmed her.

It was contagious. Together they roared with laughter until Becky was holding her sides and her mother was dabbing tears from her eyes with the back of her hand.

Finally they both subsided into sporadic, exhausted gasps. Becky sipped at her ginger ale. "Mom?" she said hesitantly.

"What?"

"Don't tell Angela. You know, about the dresses, and the dancing, and everything? I don't think she'd understand. And even if she did—well, couldn't it be private?"

"Of course it can be private. Tell you what, Beck. Let's put on our bathrobes, and I'll make some hot chocolate so we can have some with Angela when she gets home, and we can hear about her evening. And it'll be our secret, that we had our own party, and that upstairs, in the backs of our closets, we have hidden away—"

She hesitated. She stared at her own dress, and then at Becky's.

Becky finished the sentence for her. *"Splendor,"* Becky said, and grinned.

The Great Blackberry Pick

by Philippa Pearce

Do people really change? Or is it simply our way of seeing them that changes? And if we see someone differently, does that mean that we have changed?

DAD WAS AGAINST WASTE—WASTE OF ALMOST ANY-
thing: electricity, time, crusts of bread. Wasted
food was his special dread. Just after the summer
holidays, nearing the second or third Saturday of
term: "Sun now," he would say, "frost later; and
pounds and pounds and pounds and pounds of
blackberries out in the hedges going to waste.
Good food wasted: bramble jelly"—their mother
flinched, perhaps remembering stained bags hanging from hooks in the kitchen—"jelly, and jam,
and blackberry-and-apple pies...." He smacked
his lips. Dad seemed to think he must mime enjoy-
ment to make them understand.

Val said eagerly, "I love blackberries."

Her father beamed on her.

Chris said, "I don't. I don't like the seeds between my teeth."

"Worse under your plate," their mother murmured.

Like their mother, Dad had false teeth, but he
did not acknowledge them. He said scornfully, "In
bought jam the seeds are artificial. Tiny chips of
wood. Put in afterwards."

"Nice job, carving 'em to shape," said Chris.

Peter was not old enough to think that funny,
and Val decided not to laugh; so nobody did.

Peter said, "Do we have to go?"

"Bicycles," said Dad. "Everyone on bicycles and
off into the country, blackberry picking. Five of us
should gather a good harvest."

"I'll make the picnic," Val said. She liked that kind of thing. She looked anxiously around her family. Their mother had turned her face away from them to gaze out of the window. Peter and Chris had fixed their eyes upon Dad: Peter would have to go, although much bicycling made his legs ache; but Chris, the eldest of them, as good as grown-up—Chris said: "I'm not coming."

"Oh, Chris!" Val cried.

Dad said: "Not coming?"

"No."

"And why not?"

"I've been asked to go somewhere else on Saturday. I'm doing something else. I'm not coming."

No one had ever said that to Dad before. What would happen? Dad began to growl in his throat like a dog preparing to attack. Then the rumble died away. Dad said: "Oh, have it your own way then."

So that was one who wouldn't go blackberrying this year.

Nor did their mother go. When Saturday came, she didn't feel well, she said. She'd stay at home and have their supper ready for them.

Two fewer didn't matter, because Dad begged the two Turner children from next door. Mrs. Turner was glad to be rid of them for the day, and they had bicycles.

"Bicycles," said Dad, "checked in good order,

tires pumped, brakes working, and so on. Then, the picnic." Val smiled and nodded. "Something to gather the blackberries in," went on Dad. "Not paper bags or rubbishy receptacles of that sort. Baskets, plastic carrier bags, anything like that. Something that will go into a bicycle basket, or can be tied on somewhere. Something that will bear a weight of blackberries. Right?"

Val said, "Yes," so that Dad could go on: "All assemble in the road at nine thirty. I'll have the map."

There they were on this fine Saturday morning in September at half past nine: Val and Peter and their dad and the two Turner children from next door, all on bicycles.

They had about four miles on the main road, riding very carefully, two by two or sometimes in single file, with Dad in the rear shouting to them. Then Dad directed them to turn off the main road into a side road, and after that it was quiet country roads all the way. As Chris had once said, you had to hand it to Dad: Dad was good with a map; he knew where he was going.

Country roads; and then lanes that grew doubtful of themselves and became mere grassy tracks. These were the tracks that in the old days people had made on foot or on horseback, going from one village to the next. Nowadays almost no one used them.

They were pushing their bikes now, or riding them with their teeth banging in their gums. The Turner children each fell off once, and one cried.

"Quiet now!" Dad said severely, as though the blackberries were shy wild creatures to be taken by surprise.

They left their bicycles stacked against each other and followed Dad on foot, walking steeply through an afforestation of pines, and then out into a large clearing on a hillside, south-facing and overgrown with brambles.

You had to hand it to Dad; it was a marvelous place.

The bushes were often more than a man's height and densely growing, but with irregular passages between them. The pickers could edge through narrow gaps or stoop under stems arched to claw and clutch. For most of the time they wore their anoraks with the hoods up.

The blackberries grew thickly. They were very big and ripe—many already overripe, with huge bluebottles squatting on them.

"Eat what you want, to begin with," said Dad. "Soon enough you won't want to eat any more. Then just pick and go on picking." He smiled. He was good-tempered. Everything was going well.

They separated at once, to pick. They went burrowing about among the bushes, meeting each other, exclaiming, drawn to each other's blackberry clumps, because always someone else's blackberries seemed bigger, riper.

They picked and picked and picked and picked. Their teeth and tongues and lips were stained, but their fingers were stained the most deeply, because they went on picking—on and on and on—after they had stopped eating. Dad had been right about that, too. But himself, he never ate any blackberries at all; just picked.

The brambles scratched them. Val had a scratch on her forehead that brought bright blood oozing down into her eyebrow. "Nothing!" said Dad. He tied her head with a handkerchief to stop the bleeding. The handkerchief had been a present to him; it was red with white polka dots. When he had tied it round Val's head, he called her his pirate girl.

Then he looked into her plastic carrier bag. "Why, pirate girl, you've picked more blackberries than anyone else!"

When Dad had gone off again, Peter began to dance round Val: "Pirate girl! Pirate girl!" Val didn't mind; no, she really enjoyed it. She felt happy to have picked more blackberries than anyone else, and for Dad to have said so, and to be wearing Dad's handkerchief and to be teased for what he had called her. The Turner children appeared round a bramble corner, and she was glad of the audience. Peter was good-humored, too. His legs had stopped aching, and he had forgotten that they would ache again. The children were in early afternoon sunshine and blackberry-scented air; they had picked enough blackberries to be proud of; the picnic would be any time now; and Dad was in a good temper.

"Pirate girl!" Peter teased. He set down his basket of blackberries to pick a solitary stem of hogweed, dry and straight and stiff. With this he made cutlass slashes at Val.

There was no weapon near to hand for Val, so she used her carrier bag to parry him. She swung the bag to and fro, trying to bang his stem and break it. The weight in the carrier made it swing slowly, heavily, like a pendulum. Val was getting nowhere in the fight, but she was enjoying it. She hissed fiercely between her teeth. Peter dodged. The bag swung.

Dad came back round the bushes and saw them. Val couldn't stop the swinging at once; and at once an awful thing began to happen. The swinging was too much for the weight of the blackberries in the bag. The bottom did not fall out—after all, the bag was plastic; but the plastic where she gripped it began to stretch. The handle holes elongated swiftly and smoothly. Swiftly and smoothly the plastic around them thinned, thinned out into nothingness. No ripping, no violent severance; but the bag gave way.

The blackberries shot out at Dad's feet. They pattered impudently over his Wellington boots; nestled there in a squashy heap. Val, looking down at them, knew they were wasted. She had gathered them, and she had literally thrown them away. She lifted her eyes to Dad's face: his brows were heavy, his lips open and drawn back, his teeth showed, ground together.

Then he growled, in his way.

She turned and ran. She ran and ran, as fast as she could, to get away. Fast and far she ran: now, as she ran, there were pine trees on either side of her, an audience that watched her. Then she tripped and fell painfully over metal, and realized that she had reached the bicycles. She pulled her own bicycle from the heap and got on it and rode. The way was downhill and rough, and she was riding too fast for carefulness. She was shaken violently as though someone were shaking a wicked child.

She followed the track by which they had come, then diverged into another. The way grew smoother; she passed a farmhouse; the surface under her wheels was made up now. She took another turn and another, and was in a narrow road between high hedges. She cycled on and came to a crossroads: two quiet country roads quietly meeting and crossing, with no signpost saying anything. Without consideration she took the turn towards the downward sloping of the sun, and cycled on more slowly. She knew that she was lost, and she was glad of it.

She found that she had a headache. She was surprised at the headache, and wondered if the tight-tied handkerchief had caused it. Then she connected the feeling in her head with a feeling in her stomach; she was hungry. They had all been hungry for the picnic even before the pirate fight, and she had ridden away without eating.

She was so tired and hungry that she cried a little as she pedaled along. She knew she had nearly twenty pence in the pocket of her anorak. She could buy herself some food.

But these were not roads with shops on them. Another farm; a derelict cottage; and suddenly a bungalow with a notice at the gate: "Fruit. Veg."

She leaned her bicycle against the hedge and went up the path towards the front door. But the front door had a neglected look, and a power mower was parked right against it, under the shelter of the porch. She turned and went around the side of the bungalow, following a path but also a faint, enticing smell. The smell grew stronger, more exciting. The side door she came to was also a kitchen door, and it stood ajar. From inside came a smell of roast meat and of delicious baking.

Val went right up to the door and peered in. The kitchen was empty of people. A meal had just been finished. A baby's high chair stood near the table, its tray spattered with mashed potato and gravy. There was no food left on the table except more mashed potato and the remains of a treacle tart in a baking tin.

And there was the smell, overwhelming now.

Val inhaled and looked.

A door opened, and a young woman came into the kitchen. She picked up the tin with the treacle tart in it, evidently to put it away somewhere. Then she saw Val's face at the crack of the door. She gave a gasp.

Val pushed the door wide open to show how harmless she was, and with the same intention said, "I saw the notice at the gate."

"Oh," said the woman, recovering, "that shouldn't be there still. Should have come down last week. We've not much stuff left, you see. What did you want?"

"Something to eat now," said Val. The woman had put the treacle tart down on the table again.

"Blackberries?" the woman suggested.

"No," said Val. "Not blackberries. Thank you."

The woman had been staring at her. "Why's your head tied up? Have you had an accident? You're very pale."

"No," said Val. "I'm all right really." The woman's hand was still on the treacle-tart tin; she remained staring.

"You have had an accident."

"Not really." Val didn't want to think of what

had happened among the brambles. "I fell off my bike."

The woman left the treacle tart and came across to Val. She slipped the handkerchief from her head and laid it aside. She examined Val's brow. "It's really only a scratch, but it's bled a lot. You sit down." She cleaned the wound and then bandaged it. Then, "You'd better have some tea. I was going to make a pot while the baby slept." She boiled the kettle and made the tea. She also cleared the kitchen table, taking the treacle tart away and shutting it into a larder. Val watched it go, over the cup of tea the woman poured for her.

Next the woman opened the oven door just a crack. A smell of baking, hot, dry, delicious, came out and made straight for Val. The woman was peering into the oven: "Ah," she said. "Yes." She opened the oven door wide and took out two tin trays of scones, done to a turn. She got out a wire rack and began to transfer the scones one by one from the trays to the rack. They were so hot that she picked each one up by the tips of her fingers and very quickly.

"Have another cup," she said hospitably to Val.

"I won't have any more to drink, thank you," Val said. The scones sat on their wire rack, radiating heat and smell. The woman finished with the trays and began washing up.

There were footsteps outside, and a young man appeared, carrying a pig bucket. He left it just outside and came in. "Hello!" he said to Val. "Where've you sprung from?"

"She fell off her bike. I've given her a cup of tea." The woman dried her hands. "You might like a scone, too?"

Val nodded. She couldn't say anything.

The woman slit a scone, buttered it, and handed it to her.

"What about me?" asked the man.

"You!" said the woman. From the rack she chose a scone misshapen but huge, made from the last bits of dough clapped together. She slit it, pushed a hunk of butter inside, and gave it to him.

"Would you like another?" she asked Val.

Val said she would. The woman watched her eating the second scone. "Haven't you had much dinner?"

Val didn't decide what she was going to say. It came at once. "The others all rode away from me when I fell off my bike. Rode off with the picnic."

The woman was indignant. "But didn't you try to catch up with them again?"

"I got lost."

The woman gave Val a third scone and her husband a second. She went to the larder and came back with the treacle tart, which she set before Val. "There's a nice surprise for you," she said.

They asked where Val lived, and when she told them, the man said, "Quite a way on a bike."

Val said, "If you could tell me how to get to the

main road from here. All these lanes, and not many signposts . . ."

"Tricky," said the man.

Then the woman said, "Weren't you taking the van to the garage some time to get that part?"

"Ah," said the man. "Yes. I could set her on her way. Room for the bike in the back."

"No hurry," the woman said to Val. "You sit there."

Away somewhere a baby began to cry, and the woman went to fetch it. While she was out of the kitchen, the man helped himself to another scone and butter, winking at Val. The woman came back with the baby in her arms. "You!" she said to the man. He kissed her with his mouth full of scone, and kissed the baby.

The woman said to Val: "You hold her while I finish the washing-up." So Val held the baby, smelling of cream cheese and warm woollies and talcum powder. The baby seemed to like her.

"Well," the man said to Val, "I'll be back for you later."

His wife gave him the old mashed potato and other remains for the pig bucket. "It wasn't worth your coming for it specially," she said.

"No," he said. "But I remembered about the scones."

"You!" she said.

He laughed and went off with his pig bucket again.

Val nursed the baby, and gave it a rusk, and helped to change its nappies, and played with it. The mother cleared and cleaned the kitchen and washed out the nappies.

It all took some time. Then the man came again. "Ready?" he said to Val. Val took her anorak, which the baby had been sucking, and went with him. He had already hoisted the bicycle into the back of the van. The woman came to the gate with the baby in her arms. The baby slapped at the notice saying: "Fruit. Veg." "You never get around to taking that notice down," the woman said to her husband. He grunted, busy with the van. Val kissed good-bye to the baby, who took a piece of her cheek and twisted it.

Then Val got into the van and they drove off. Val was not noticing the way they took; she was thinking of the warm, sweet-smelling kitchen they had left. As they drove along, she half-thought they passed one of the two farmhouses she had noticed earlier when she was cycling; but that was all.

She began to think of what it would be like when she got home.

They reached the main road at last and drove along it a short way to the garage. Here the man lifted Val's bicycle out of the van, and she mounted it. He gave her clear directions to set her on her way, ending with, "You should be home well before dusk."

So she was; and they were all waiting for her. Even Chris was there. The Turner children had wanted to stay, too, but Dad had packed them off home.

There was a great explosion from Dad about what had happened at the blackberry pick and after. Val was given some supper, but the row from Dad went on during it and after it. Their mother started her ironing; Chris settled down to TV; Peter played a quiet but violent game with soldiers and tanks behind the couch. Dad went on and on.

"And what about that bandage?" he shouted suddenly. Their mother knocked the iron against the ironing board, almost toppling it. "Where's my red handkerchief that I lent you?"

In a flash of memory Val saw the red handkerchief laid aside on the dresser in that scone-smelling, baby-smelling kitchen. "A woman gave me a cup of tea," she said. "She took the handkerchief off and put the bandage on instead. I must have left the handkerchief there."

"My red handkerchief!" Dad shouted.

"Oh," muttered Chris, without taking his eyes off TV, "a red cotton handkerchief!"

"I'm sorry," Val said to Dad.

"Sorry!"

Then Dad cross-questioned her. Who was this woman, and where did she live? All Val could say was that she lived quite a way from the bramble patch and from the main road, in a bungalow with a notice at the gate saying: "Fruit. Veg."

"Right," said Dad. "You'll come with me tomorrow. You'll cycle back the way you came. You'll help me search until we find that bungalow and the woman and my red handkerchief."

So the next day—Sunday—Val cycled with her father alone into the country. Just the two of them: once she would have loved that.

He led them systematically to and fro among the country lanes. ("Do you recognize this road? Could that be the bungalow? Look, girl, *look!*") Dad knew his map, and he was thorough in his crisscrossing of the countryside; but they saw few bungalows, and none with a notice at the gate saying: "Fruit. Veg."

As they passed one bungalow, Val looked up the path to the front door. Against it under the shelter of the porch was parked a motor mower. Also a pole with a board at the top; the inscription on the board faced the front door. And behind the glass of a window Val thought she saw movement—the odd, top-heavy shape of someone carrying a child. But they were cycling past too quickly for her to be sure.

When they got home at last, Dad was too tired to go on with the row. He just said: "A day wasted!"

Val was even more tired; and she said nothing.

The Snakeskin Bag

by Constance C. Greene

One difference between strangers and people we're used to is that strangers don't know our rules. Some newcomers catch on quickly. Others make their own rules....

THE NEW GIRL IS FROM TENNESSEE, WHICH SHE SAYS IS much nicer than here. Her bright hair tickles her backside and her shocking-pink skirt whirls around her as she walks. Her eyes are shaded lavender to match her blouse. But the best thing about her is her ladies'-size handbag. She carries it carefully, switching it from one shoulder to the other constantly, as if it holds her life savings. Or as if it's full of gold. Or pieces of eight.

"My ma made it." She rolls her eyes at her handbag. "It's real snakeskin. First she catches the snake," and she shows with her hands how her ma catches the snake, "then she strangles it with one twist," and she shows the exact way her ma twists the snake to strangle it, "then she turns it into things she makes for her boutique." She pronounces it "bow-tique."

Oh yeah! Sure! You bet! greets this. But they don't go away.

"Children, this is Anna Voss," the teacher says. "Please make her welcome. Help her to settle in."

"Help her settle in!" Margie Palamountain spits out. "She's already settled in like a hen on a nest. Help her settle in!"

"Most folks call me Pretty," the new girl says, grinning all around. She's the only girl in the class wearing a skirt. That doesn't seem to bother her like it would most. The others wear jeans and T-shirts with things written on them: "Your Mother Wears GI Shoes" or "I Brake for Cute Boys."

123

She almost died of Rocky Mountain spotted fever this very summer, the new girl says. "Seventeen ticks in all," and she shows them where the ticks were located. "I cut 'em out with these," and she dives into her bag and comes up with garden shears with orange handles. "Those ticks, see, they dig in and grab ahold, and shoot off their poison," she says, cheeks flaming, hair crackling. "If you don't dig 'em out straightaway, they kill you right off." She looks around, her eyes glittering with truth.

"Most folks die of the spotted fever," she whispers so everyone has to lean close to hear every word.

Margie Palamountain is beside herself. She shouts, "My dog had Rocky Mountain spotted fever and *he* didn't die!" Margie is in one of her famous huffs. "Folks don't get spotted fever. Only dogs do." Margie has a way of saying things that folks don't argue with.

The new girl doesn't even look in Margie's direction. She just opens her bag up a slit so anyone can have a peek. Inside is a hairbrush bristling with bright hairs and a flat silver case.

"For my cigs," the new girl says, tapping a finger against the case. "Camels," she says, and her eyes crinkle up and she laughs.

"Give us a look!" Leroy Macy calls out. Leroy has big horn-rimmed glasses and the highest IQ in the class. Leroy plans on going to business school, and after, he plans on selling feed and grain at his daddy's store. Leroy's mama's papa is president of the bank. Every year he gets a new car which he drives slowly back and forth in front of his bank so folks can see their money is in good hands.

The new girl wears sneakers and no socks. Flesh-colored hose is what she wears, she says. Margie Palamountain drops her pencil box and when she bends down to pick it up, she accidentally brushes against the new girl's leg.

"That is skin," Margie says later in the girls' room, her mouth tucked into a tight little knot. "That is no hose, flesh-color or otherwise. That is purely skin."

Leroy Macy wears his good blue suit three days in a row. At recess, a crowd gathers round the new girl and there is a lot of noisy laughter. Leroy's voice gets very loud and his eyebrows rattle around on his forehead, which is what happens when Leroy gets excited.

He talks a lot about his IQ and how it seems to keep going up. Nobody knows why. He tells about his mama's diamond rings that she brings out of her safety deposit box in her daddy's bank every Christmas Eve. Leroy also says he might travel to Washington at spring vacation in his granddaddy's car. He might ask some friends to go along, he says, pushing his glasses up on his nose and rattling his eyebrows some more.

They might see the President, Leroy hints.

Margie Palamountain says she has never heard so many tall tales in all her life.

The new girl swings her snakeskin bag in wider and wider circles around her head. The boys hoot and holler and duck, following the track the bag takes, making bets as to whether or not she'll let slip and the bag will escape. They try to stay out of her way by getting closer to her.

Except for Leroy, who just stands there, goggle-eyed.

The bag nails him. On his head. The blood runs down into his eyes. And onto his good blue suit. Everybody starts screaming.

"Stand back," the new girl says. "My ma's a nurse and I know what to do." She kneels down next to Leroy, who is bleeding all over the playground.

"Keep still," she tells him, as if he wasn't already still. Somebody runs to get the nurse, who is also the gym teacher and fills in for the English teacher when the English teacher gets sick.

The nurse comes roaring out.

"Don't touch him!" the nurse yells. "I'll handle this."

The new girl puts her garden shears with the orange handles back into her bag. She has taken them out while kneeling over Leroy. Lucky for him there's so much blood dripping into his eyes he can't see the shears. Leroy's glasses are broken. He feels his nose. Maybe it's broken too, he says.

"It wasn't my fault," the new girl says. "He got in the way. It wasn't my fault." For the first time, she stops smiling.

Leroy has to have ten stitches in his head. His daddy is fit to be tied. Leroy's mama is likewise. Leroy's granddaddy threatens to sue.

"It was an accident," the principal says. "Nobody's fault, an accident is all."

The new girl doesn't bring the snakeskin bag to school again.

It's a blessing Leroy didn't lose his eyesight. That's what Margie Palamountain says. More than once, too. Margie thinks Leroy should sue even if he didn't lose his eyesight. Leroy will probably be scarred for life, Margie says.

The day after the accident, the new girl comes to school in a dress made of black taffeta. A bow-tique item, she says. A big seller. Nobody has ever seen, much less heard of, such a thing as black taffeta. She whispers when she walks. But the bag is not there. No snakeskin bag with her cigs in their flat silver case and the garden shears with the orange handles. And the hairbrush bristling with bright hairs. All gone.

Leroy sticks to the new girl's side as if he's pasted there, goggle-eyed as ever. She pays him no mind but her eyes flash at him now and then, just enough to keep him anxious.

In no time, the new girl says she's moving back to Tennessee. Plans for her mother's bow-tique, she says, haven't worked out. Besides, her mother's getting married to a rich cowboy who not only has a lot of cows, he also has a Cadillac agency. He must sell about a thousand Cadillacs a year, she says, licking her lips.

"There is nothing he wouldn't do for us," the new girl says, eyelids drooping, concealing her eyes. "Nothing is too good for us, he says." She looks up and her eyes glisten. "He says he loves us with all his heart."

No one has ever before heard such words spoken. Their mouths drop open, their feet are still.

"My ma says that's worth a fortune, right there. To be loved by all someone's heart, my ma says, is money in the bank."

She crosses her arms on her chest. And is silent.

Who else can say that? To be loved with all of anyone's heart must be the most wonderful thing in the world.

In a loud voice, Margie Palamountain says her uncle sent her two rolls of quarters for her to play the slot machines next time she goes to where they have slot machines.

"We might go by bus," Margie says. "We might stay in a hotel. With a floor show."

A sigh goes up.

The new girl swings her arms wide, ever wider. But there is nothing there. They are empty. She lets her arms drop to her side.

"And chorus girls," Margie throws in for good measure.

In a matter of days, the new girl is gone. It is as if she's never been. If it wasn't for Leroy's stitches, which are healing nicely, she might've been a dream. Or even a ghost.

Leroy is very glum, his eyebrows never still.

Margie Palamountain says the new girl was plenty real.

"Didn't I feel her leg?" Margie says in a hoarse voice. "That was real skin. That was no flesh-color hose. That was purely skin," Margie says triumphantly. She lets her voice drop.

"And what about the bag?"

Nobody argues with Margie.

Shoes

by John Wideman

Is it possible to know someone you've never met, and to remember someone you never knew?

[Guam is an island in the Pacific where there was fighting during World War II. A lithographed Pietà is a copy of a painting that shows Jesus' mother, Mary, weeping over his crucified body.]

THIS IS ABOUT A BOY AND A PAIR OF SHOES. NOT really, but one thing is as good as another for the first suspension of disbelief.

Once upon a time there was a gym. A sweaty gym where games were played and time passed with little pain. Eugene played basketball there and was good at it. Because he was strong, fast, and loved to feel the oil of his body slick and rich on his skin, although he didn't think of the last of these things. He was loud and stubborn, and these qualities grew up with him to become manly confidence. But not too long, because Eugene didn't grow too long, cut down by a Japanese bayonet on Guam after twenty years of life. That's his story, or at least as much of his story as I know because most of Eugene happened before I was born. You see, he was my uncle, and not talked of much by the time I could listen. I suppose it's just as well, because I knew him better through his shoes.

They were huge. Dusty under the bed, found one morning while searching for dragons. I dragged them out like barges and stepped into them, shoes and all. They made me feel colossus-tall, stretched over two worlds. They had been waiting, the way she still waited each morning at the gate, early, because she knew he would return just as the sun rose. The rest of him had been packed or given away after a decent interval, but this canvas-and-rubber had been missed—or perhaps she meant to miss them. They were grass-stained and dry. Sweat had dyed them brown along the seams, and what had probably been mud crumbled dustily from where it had caked on the instep and laces. Probably football. A long, high pass, perfect as a bird, and he with his legs flying to hawk it in. A scramble, but your fingers are quicker, tougher, and you have it. Touchdown!

How easy, how uncomprehending it was. Afternoons loud and clear. But Eugene is dead—died with his boots on—in another field, another muddy gutted island, where people thought differently.

She remembers how out on the roof the shoes would go, because "I don't want them things smellin' up the house." He would be insulted, but after pouting awhile it was more fun to join the others laughing. How those rings he left in the tub seemed painted on.

It's too easy—too pure, pat. Her story. It's too old, too sad—mothers weeping on the plains of Troy, the beaches of Normandy, at the foot of a cross. A Pietà, lithographed, that lines a drawer. Besides, a pair of shoes have been lived in—no reason for regret.

"Oh Mary don't you weep;
tell Martha not to moan"

And the rest tells why, but I remember only the music.

Maybe you've heard it anyway. She did. She did and stopped those morning walks to the gate. And the shoes grew smaller.

I was the one who couldn't let go. Knowing little else perhaps was why the shoes wouldn't leave my mind. But they left the house, and I remember how alone it felt to be kneeling in front of the closet with piles of shoes pulled out around me and finding them not there. I thought of going out into the yard, looking in the garbage can, rescuing and hiding them in some secret place—like I had hidden the shell of the turtle who had died and was buried which I dug up again to hold my favorite marbles—cats' eyes, crystals, agates—that rattled like false teeth in the scooped-out shell. But the cans stood near the gate; I would be seen from the kitchen rummaging around and told to go away or, worse, asked what I was doing—and I didn't know because the shoes were just things that I liked; things that started to mean something, but never let me get close enough long enough to ask why.

133

Anyway, they couldn't talk because they were shoes, and if they could, whatever they said would smell of mud, sweat, grass, and blood . . .

Still, I walked and ran in them many times after. Not so big now, because they had grown smaller; but I was bigger, much bigger, than when I couldn't find them to wear. Once I thought I heard them as they tried to speak. Surprisingly there was no gruffness. Rather, a gentle voice, like a lullaby, or a balloon losing its air slowly.

Of him, she spoke gently, too. Would even say his name softly when others were listening, or smile as the conversation lit momentarily on his shoulders. It was at dinner—in autumn, because I remember hearing something shuffle through the high piles of leaves we had pushed along the sides of the path outside the window—that one of those infrequent questions was asked of me.

"Do you remember your Uncle Eugene?"

The leaves shouted at me and I couldn't raise my voice over their noise. I was sure now I heard a clump, clump muffled step moving down the path towards the gate.

"Do you remember your Uncle Eugene?"

They laughed now, a bunch of big boys laughing at all they knew I didn't know, leaves laughing because he was walking among them.

"Do you hear me?"

And I cried because I knew no one heard, and no welcome but the vacant shuffling of the leaves would greet him.

"Don't frighten the boy, of course he's too young to remember."

It shut and he never came back and I knew he wouldn't and cried deeper, but the tears stopped and the forks and knives rang louder and the leaves drifted silently like sand to fill the holes he had made.

Your Mind Is a Mirror

by Joan Aiken

Which is the more difficult journey—from Greece to
London, from now to yesterday, or from lonely brood-
ing grief to shared sorrow?

A KEEN WIND SCOURED THE DECK OF THE FERRY SHIP
Colossos, probing between the slats of the wooden
seats on the upper section, making the passengers
huddle together, pull on cardigans if they had
them, or go below for cups of hot coffee. Mist was
beginning to veil the Turkish coast on the left-
hand side, and blur the shapes of the islands to the
right. Another hour must pass before the ship
docked in Rhodes. Sam and Linnet wrapped their
bare legs in their swimming towels, but a damp
swimming towel is very poor protection against a
cold searching wind. They had begged for a last
swim and Ma had said, "Oh, very well! Meet us at
the dock, and promise you won't be a minute later
than half past twelve. But that means you'll have
to wear beach clothes on the boat, because your
other clothes will be packed."

"Doesn't matter," Sam had said. "It'll be hot."

But it wasn't hot; the weather had turned misty
and windy. "Most unlike the Aegean at this time of
year," other passengers were grumbling. The
Palmers' luggage was at the very bottom of a huge
heap of bags and crates on the lower deck; impossible to dig down to their rucksacks and get out
warmer clothes. All their books were packed, too;
there was nothing to do but sit and shiver, for the
boat was jam-packed with tourists, mainly Swedes
and Germans; you couldn't even walk about to
keep yourself warm, because there wasn't a foot of
spare deck space. Sam did his best to doze a bit; he

had woken very early and listened to the crowing of roosters near and far, anxious not to miss a minute of their last day on Kerimos. But it was too cold on the boat for proper sleeping; he had a brief, sad dream about his dear French teacher who had died, Madame Bonamy.

When he shook himself awake, Father was sitting staring ahead in silence, as usual, and Ma was murmuring something to Linnet in a low anxious voice.

In several ways it had been a miserable holiday. The tiny Greek island was beautiful, of course; the little Greek house with its bare painted floors, basic wooden furniture, and garden full of roses and lemons, had been perfect; the swimming in a clear green sea, the cliffs covered with rockroses, the village that was all steps up and steps down, dazzling white houses, ancient crumbling churches, and flowers everywhere—every detail of that had been marvellous, wonderful, but Father had spoiled it. Silent, grim, day after day, he had sat in one place, generally the darkest corner of the darkest room indoors, unless Ma had urged him to go out, when he had shrugged and slouched out to the garden as if it did not matter to him where he moved his load of misery. On excursions, or when they ate dinner out at one of the tavernas on the quayside, he had accompanied his wife and children like an angry, speechless ghost.

Why should he object if we are enjoying our-
selves? thought Sam resentfully. We aren't doing
him any harm.

Possibly Father didn't really notice whether
thcy wcre enjoying themselves or not; he never
looked at the other three members of his family,
just stared off into the distance like an Easter Island statue on the side of a hill. His wife and children shared plain, nondescript looks: Sam and
Linnet had straight brown hair, snub noses, freck-
les, and greyish brown eyes; Ma had a pleasant
friendly face, but it was always worried nowadays
which made it almost ugly; she didn't bother about
clothes or make-up much any more, and her hair
was badly in need of a perm, it looked like a piece
of knitting that had gone wrong. Father had always been the handsome member of the family,
with his classically straight forehead and nose, all
in one line, his bright brown hair and beard, now
just touched with grey, and bright dark twinkling
grey eyes. But now his eyes had ceased to twinkle;
they stared into the distance, hour after hour, day
after day, as if nothing nearby had the power to
please them. Once, his conversation had been full
of jokes and interesting information; now, often, a
whole day would pass without his speaking at all
except to say "I don't mind."

"Would you rather have a boiled egg or scrambled, Jonathan?" Ma would ask at breakfast.

"Do you want to watch BBC or ITV?"

"Shall we go to Brighton to see Fanny, or for a walk on the Heath?"

"I don't mind."

In the end, Ma hadn't even bothered to consult him about the holiday on Kerimos; she sold some shares Granny had left her, bought the tickets, rented the house, and packed Father's bag for him. He hadn't raised any objections. But for all the good that sun and sea and Greek air had done him, he might as well have stayed at home in Camden Town.

"You do realise he's sick, don't you?" Ma had said anxiously to Sam.

"How do you mean, sick? Has he got a pain, is something wrong with him?"

Sickness to Sam meant medicine, hospitals, bandages, injections.

"His mind is sick. He's depressed, because he was let go, because he can't get a teaching job anywhere. And he's such a good teacher—"

Sam couldn't see it. Lots of the boys at school had unemployed parents, who grumbled and moaned, of course, worried about money, were hopeful of jobs or disappointed when the hopes came to nothing; but in between times they seemed reasonably cheerful, mowed their lawns, took the family to the movies once in a while, didn't retreat into this marble staring world of silence. Why did Jonathan Palmer have to be different?

An extra-keen gust of wind worked its way under Sam's thin T-shirt and he shivered.

"Brr, I'm freezing!"

"So am I," sighed Linnet.

Their father's indifferent gaze passed right over them, as if they had spoken in Hindustani, but Ma said, "Here, you two, here's a couple of hundred drachmae. You'd better go and buy yourselves a coffee. And bring some back for me and Father. I'll stay here. . . ."

"I wonder if she thinks he might jump over the side," murmured Linnet, shivering as they stood in line at the coffee counter.

Sam muttered, "I hate Dad. I really hate him. I almost wish he would jump over the side."

"Oh, Sam. You know it's just that he's ill. And think how hard it must have been for him losing his job, when Ma's still teaching at the same school. He just isn't himself. Remember! He never used to be like this."

"Well, why can't he go back to the way he used to be?" Sam said disbelievingly.

"People can't get better just by wanting to."

"Well then he ought to go to a shrink."

"Costs money. And the Health Service shrinks have waiting-lists as long as the Milky Way." Linnet paid for the coffee and looked frustratedly at the huge pile of baggage. "I do wish we could get our books out and read."

Sam fingered the beach satchel under his arm. As well as damp swimming trunks, flippers, and snorkel mask, it contained a guilty secret.

Several times, swimming from the tiny town beach, they had noticed a Greek family group who attracted Sam's attention because they seemed in every way the converse of the Palmers. There were two lively handsome dark brothers, older; two small pretty sisters, younger; there was a fat cheerful aunt, a plump smiling mother, and above all, there was a talkative, ebullient father who seemed the king-pin of the whole tribe, affectionate with the girls, companionable and teasing with the boys, bounding in and out of the water, rushing away to the quay and returning with almond cakes, ice-creams, and fruit; sweeping the family off to eat lunch at quayside tavernas, and all the time making jokes, laughing, hugging his wife, complimenting his sister-in-law, carrying the smaller girl piggyback up the rocky path. If only Father could be like that! Had he ever been?

Sam could hardly remember the days before Jonathan Palmer's illness; the mist of unhappiness that surrounded him seemed to block out any view of the past.

On this final morning the Greek father had produced from his pocket a little book, a glossy paperback, from which he proceeded to read aloud, amid bursts of general hilarity. At every paragraph, almost every sentence he read, his wife, children, and sister-in-law collapsed and beat their chests in hiccups of laughter. Sam could feel a smile break out over his own face at the sight and sound of so much happy humour. Then, gaily, impulsively, forgetting the book, leaving their swimming things scattered on the sand, they had all gone bounding off to the nearest quayside cafe for coffee and cakes. Linnet was still in the sea, making the most of her last swim, nobody else on the beach was anywhere near; Sam had walked casually past, casually dropped his towel, and picked up towel and book together. Why? He hardly knew himself. Perhaps the book was a kind of token, a talisman, a spell, a magic text that would bring fun and good humour back into his own family if he read it aloud?

There had been no chance to look inside the book since he picked it up; Linnet had dashed out of the sea, they had dressed and sprinted round to the berth where the *Colossos* waited at her moorings. But now Sam could feel the paperback, a small, encouraging rectangular shape, wrapped in a plastic bag between his trunks and towel. He would study it tonight when they were back at home, though now it seemed almost impossible to believe that by bedtime they would be in their own

143

house, in Camden Town, the island of Kerimos, with its white houses and turquoise sea, nothing but a bright memory.

Home, when they reached it, smelt shut-in and stuffy; Ma went round at once throwing open windows. Father sat down, just as he was, without even pulling off his windcheater, in a chair by the fireplace, and stared, unseeing, at the unlit gas fire. Home smelt of all the sorrow that had ever happened there. . . .

But here was fat Simon, Sam's cat, a plump sharply striped young tabby, half frantic with pent-up affection, wanting to be picked up, rolling on his back to have his stomach rubbed, leaping onto Sam's lap at every possible and impossible moment, miaowing and purring nonstop and simultaneously to indicate his displeasure at having been left to the care of neighbours for two solid weeks.

"I don't believe a word of what you say!" Sam told him. "You aren't starved, fat cat Simon— you're even fatter than you were when we left. You should see some of those skinny Greek cats, you spoilt thing."

The island had been full of cats, healthy and active but thin as diagrams; they waited hungrily and acrimoniously for fishbones around every quayside cafe.

Sam raced up to his room with Simon wailing

two steps behind him, flung his rucksack on the bed, then pulled the stolen book from his beach satchel and eagerly opened it.

The disappointment was shattering; there were no pictures in the book, and (as he might have considered if he had given it a moment's thought) the text was all in Greek, in Greek characters; he could read no more than a word here and there, *kai* for "and," *alla* for "but." He had committed theft, he had stolen a book, the book that had given them all such joy, and it was no use to him, no use at all. Guilt began to rise up in him like bubbles in jam that has started to ferment and go bad. He felt sick with dismay and horror at what he had done.

"Sam, you're tired out," said Ma, looking at him acutely when he came downstairs with a load of dirty clothes for the machine. "Off you go, straight to bed. It's too late for supper. Lin's gone up already."

Father had not gone to bed. He sat on, staring at the dead fire; he often sat that way all night.

"Good night, Father," Sam called, but did not expect, or receive, any answer.

Sam dragged himself up the stairs to bed, feeling as if he had travelled three times, on hands and knees, round the world. His only comfort (but that a substantial one, he must admit) was fat cat Simon, lovingly shoving himself as close to Sam's chin as he could squeeze.

Sam fell asleep and began to dream instantly.

There was Madame Bonamy, half stern, half smiling, as she often had been, her white wild hair standing up in a corona all round her head, elegantly tilted on its long neck, her deep-set dark eyes watchful on either side of an aquiline nose, her mouth set in a firm line.

Madame Bonamy had been quite young, in her thirties; illness, not age, had turned her hair white. Her skin was smooth but completely colourless; that, and the fine thistledown white hair, had given her the look of a ghost long before she became one. She did not behave like a ghost, then or in Sam's dreams. As a teacher she had been very funny, used to tell zany, crazy stories, and dry, ironic ones which packed a terrific punch, so it was worth listening to them carefully. Her students always came out top in French exams. For several years she had been a great friend of the Palmers'. Jonathan and his wife both taught at the same school, where Sam and Linnet were pupils, and Madame Bonamy often came to their house for meals, or joined them on family excursions, before she went into hospital for the last time and died.

"Why do people have to get ill? Why do they have to lose their jobs?" Sam asked her now, in his dream.

But Madame Bonamy did not answer his question. She had something of her own to say.

"Ah, Sam, why, why did you do it? *Non, non, non, ce n'est pas gentil!* That was a wrong thing to do, you know well. You must give it back. You should not have taken it."

"Give it *back?*" he said, appalled. "But—how can I? That family are on a Greek island—on Kerimos—six hours' journey from here. How can I possibly take it back? I don't know their name—I can't even post it to them. They probably didn't live on the island—they were on holiday too. . . ."

"Sam, Sam, why did you take it?"

He tried to explain. "It was such a funny book— it was making them all laugh so much—I thought—I thought perhaps it might make Father laugh, if it was so funny. You ought to understand that," he told her.

"Ah, I see." She reflected in silence for a moment. Then she told Sam, "Well, it is still possible for you to return it. That will mean going into the past."

"Into the past? How in the world can I do that?"

"You must go back precisely to the point at which you took the book. Not a moment sooner, not a moment later. Put the book down on the beach where you picked it up."

"How can I get there?"

"You go backwards," explained Madame Bonamy. "That is not difficult. Write with this diamond pencil on the looking-glass. Write very

147

small. First, place the book under the glass—so."

Sam, who had got out of bed, took the diamond pencil from her and stood before the mirror on the dressing-table. Simon the cat, uncurling himself, yawning, stretching, followed Sam.

"What shall I write?"

"You must write in backwards writing, beginning at the bottom right-hand corner. Each word back to front. Each sentence back to front. You must write everything that you did, every single thing that you have done today, backwards, beginning at the last minute before you got into bed."

"I see." Sam thought for a minute, then lifted his hand towards the glass.

"Attendez un moment," said Madame Bonamy. "This is important. As soon as you have replaced the book on the beach, *come straight back;* it is possible to come back very fast, as if you were quickly rewinding a tape. Do not linger for a single instant."

"Why not?"

"To go back, just for an instant like that, does not part the strands of time," said Madame Bonamy. "But if you stayed even a few moments longer, you would begin making differences, having effects on future events. Also, you might get lost."

The very thought made him shiver.

Quickly he began to write on the glass.

"Let me think then . . . I brushed my teeth; I took off my clothes; I came upstairs; I said goodnight to Father; I took the clothes down to Ma; I looked at the book; I put my rucksack down on my bed; I fed Simon; I helped get the bags out of the taxi . . ."

Minute by minute he navigated back through the long day, and each minute in its turn was recorded in tiny, spidery silver writing from right to left across the face of the mirror. At last Sam came to the point of recording: "I stooped and picked up the book and the towel both together."

And *there he was*, back on the cool, sunny beach, clouds already beginning faintly to mist over the sun, stooping down with the glossy paperback in his hand.

He laid it neatly where it had been before, and straightened, looking about him, with an immense lightening of the heart.

One thing at least had been put right; one thing need trouble him no longer.

But then, with a shock of utter dismay, he felt fat Simon rubbing possessively against his leg. Fat cat Simon, who had no right in the world to be there on a Greek beach on the island of Kerimos!

And next minute one of the quayside cats, a thin, raggedy black tom, howled out such a frightful piece of insulting cat language from the concrete steps close by, where they were building a new cafe, that fat Simon, insulted beyond bearing, shot after the black cat in a flash, there was a flurry, a scurry, black and tabby fur flew about, and both cats vanished, yowling and spitting, under a half-built boat.

"*Simon!* Come back here!" shouted Sam in horror, and darted up the steps after his cat. But, hunt though he might all over the quay, his cat was nowhere to be found. There were dozens and dozens of crannies and corners where the two cats might have retired to carry on their dispute: up alleyways, under stalls, under boats, in crowded little food shops, or under the tablecloths and benches of tavernas. The search almost at once began to seem utterly hopeless.

And all the time he could hear the voice of Madame Bonamy saying, *come straight back.* He knew he should not be there, that Simon should not be there. He did not dare speak to anybody, ask if they had seen his cat. Was he already parting the strands of time, by searching and calling?

Oh, if only Madame Bonamy were there!

I mustn't stay here in Kerimos by myself, he thought wretchedly. But to leave Simon here— how could he do that? What could he do?

Then a hopeful idea slid into his mind. Wild, maybe, but hopeful. If it were possible to go back earlier still—go back to a time *before* the Kerimos holiday—before Simon was lost . . .

But how to do that, without the diamond, without the mirror?

Standing in miserable indecision, looking across the brilliant blue water of the harbour at the white houses on the far side, Sam heard the echo of another voice, remembered from long ago.

"Your mind is a mirror; your mind is a mirror reflecting the world, showing you the image of the world around you, and all you have ever seen in it."

Who had said that?

Never mind who said it, *it was true!* My mind is a mirror, Sam thought; I can write on it. I have to remember all that has happened to me, from taking the book, back and back and farther back, like unwinding a tape . . .

And, thinking hard, thinking for his very life, he began to remember.

Minute by minute he travelled back, and as he grew more expert at remembering, the minutes zipped by faster and faster, while he guided himself through the past with the skill of a skater or a wind-surfer, steering towards marker buoys, watching out for mileposts as they flashed up and past him. There was the time Linnet broke her leg; the time the chimney blew off in a gale; the time he lost his watch; the time they had the French boy, Pierre, to stay; the time Granny came for Christmas; the time he and Linnet had measles—stop! *That* had been when Dad gave him Simon as a kitten to cheer up a miserable convalescence, when his ears ached, and his glands were all swelled up, and Linnet went back to school and he was still stuck in bed.

Stop! he ordered the minutes, and they whirled to a flashing conclusion and left him in his own bed, in his own room in Camden Town, and there was Father, as he used to be, undoing a square cat-basket with holes in the sides to reveal a roly-poly grey-and-black-striped kitten, who displayed no sort of anxiety or homesickness but leapt confidently straight onto Sam's bed, and burrowed and trod himself a comfortable nest under the feather quilt.

"Measles medicine," said Sam's father, smiling, "to help you pass the time till you're allowed to read again."

"Oh, Dad!"

Being deprived of books had been the worst part of measles.

"It's so boring lying in bed doing nothing," Sam had complained, and Dad said—yes, yes, it was Dad who had said it—"Your mind is a mirror, reflecting the world. Look into your mind and you can find any image that it has ever held. You can always find something there to think about, to entertain yourself."

Dad had said it.

"Can I come up?" called a familiar voice from downstairs. *"Est-ce qu'on peut entrer?"* and Madame Bonamy came into the bedroom carrying a pile of books. "Yes, yes, I know that you are not permitted to read, Sam, but I have come to read *to* you, so pay attention. Mary gives permission for this visit. *Allô,* Jonathan, *mon vieux,* have you heard the story about the horseman and the oysters?"

And in no time she and Sam's father were swapping lunatic tales and laughing their heads off, and Sam showed Madame Bonamy his new kitten, burrowed under the quilt, and Ma had come up with a pot of tea and cups and a big mug of orange juice for Sam; it had been a memorably happy afternoon.

"Madame Bonamy," said Sam swiftly when there was a break in the talk, "I have to ask you something. I'm all tangled up in time, things just couldn't be worse or more complicated. Simon is going to be lost on Kerimos—how will I ever get him back?"

He would have liked to ask about Father, too— how to unlock him, how to get him out of the marble prison—but how could that be done with Dad right in the room there, and Ma pouring tea? As it was, Sam's parents gave him puzzled looks, and Ma said, "Are you running a temperature again, Sam? Going to be lost on Kerimos, whatever are you talking about?"

But Madame Bonamy appeared to understand Sam and she answered, "Cats are not subject to time quite as humans are, Sam, so perhaps you need not despair. Also there is a lucky charm with cats that I have sometimes used. When you walk up the hill on your way to school, count the cats in the front gardens as you go by—"

"Oh yes, I've often done that! If you get as far as nine, it's a lucky day."

"So; no need to instruct you, I see," she said, smiling. "You have discovered for yourself how to undo the time chain."

Then she read aloud a French play to Sam, and his parents, though protesting that they ought to be correcting exam books, had stayed and taken parts; everyone had laughed at their bad pronunciation, and Madame Bonamy carefully tore a slip of paper from her notebook and inscribed a Z on it. "For the worst French accent in the country," she said, giving it to Jonathan Palmer. "Well," he objected, "I teach physics, not French, what do you expect?" But Madame Bonamy said she knew the rudiments of physics as well as French; one ought to extend the range of one's knowledge as wide as possible, she said. "It is never too late to learn."

Then she had left, calling from the stairs that she would let herself out and hoped to see Sam in class again next week. Sam wondered at the time why his mother gave Madame Bonamy such a loving, intent look; full of admiration yet sorrowful too, like that of an older sister who knows the troubles the younger one will have to meet. Later, Sam thought he understood that look.

Was that the last time Madame Bonamy had come to the house? It had been a long, long time ago.

Thinking these thoughts, Sam became aware that he was sitting up in bed, that he was awake, at home in Camden Town, and that the night was nearly over, the grey light of dawn filtering in at the windows.

Good heavens. Had he dreamed the whole thing? Madame Bonamy, and her advice, and the journey back in time to Kerimos, the journey even farther back in time, to this very room?

Which layer of time was he occupying now?

Rather tremulous, feeling hollow and strange, as if his legs had been walking hundreds of miles while he was asleep, Sam got out of bed and tip-toed across to the dressing-table, to the mirror. Nothing was written on its surface: no faint, spidery, silvery backwards handwriting—there was nothing to be seen but his own anxious face, pale and smudge-eyed, staring back at him from the glass.

But the book that had lain under the mirror was gone.

And, search as he might through his scattered belongings, and all over the room, Sam could not find it.

Fat cat Simon was gone too. Which was worrying: dreadfully worrying. True, the window was open, and Simon often did go out, via the branches of a plum tree, towards the end of the night, on his own concerns; but how to be sure of that? Suppose he was still left behind, fighting the wild black cat on Kerimos?

But—wait a minute, wait a minute—what had Madame Bonamy said about that? About cats?

Hastily, but trying to be as quiet as a ghost because it was still very, very early—yesterday at this time he would have been listening to the crowing of Greek roosters—no town traffic was abroad yet, no trains passing, no milk bottles clattering—Sam scrambled into his clothes and stole downstairs. He simply had to be sure about Simon, he could not bear another minute's uncertainty.

On his way to the front door he stopped, with a gulp that seemed to shift his heart on its foundations, at the sight of his father, Jonathan, still sitting, wide awake, silent and staring, in the front room, as he must have sat all night long.

"Oh—hallo, Dad," Sam gasped in a whisper, but trying to make his voice sound as ordinary as possible. "I—I got up early. I'm just—just going out to look for Simon."

His father's eyes moved in their sockets and regarded Sam; they held a vaguely puzzled expression.

"Dad," burst out Sam irrepressibly, "do you re-

156

member once saying that your mind is a mirror? That you can look into it and see anything in the world, anything in the past? Do you remember that?"

Jonathan's eyes seemed to become even more puzzled; then there emerged a soft sound from him as if he were trying out his throat, preparing to speak.

"Do you remember, Dad," Sam went on in a rush, "do you remember an afternoon when Madame Bonamy came and read a French play to me, and gave you a Z mark for your bad pronunciation? It was the day you brought me Simon."

Slowly, as if movements were not something he was used to, Jonathan pulled out a wallet from his breast pocket and began awkwardly and hesitantly thumbing through its contents. At last, from the very back, he pulled out a grimy slip of paper, on which was inscribed in ink a large flourishing capital Z.

He held out the paper; the eyes of father and son met over it, and both smiled, just a little.

Then Jonathan spoke, in a rusty whisper.

"Where—er—where did you say that you were going?"

"Out to look for Simon. He's missing. I shan't be gone long, I hope," Sam asserted stoutly, trying to sound confident and cheerful. "When I come back I'll put on the kettle for a cup of tea."

And he walked out into the cool grey city dawn. Far off he could hear the voice of industry beginning to stir and rumble. But here, in this elderly residential neighbourhood, all was quiet.

Cats were out in gardens, though; Sam saw the marmalade tom across the street, and the slinky grey from next door, and the dirty black-and-white in the garden two houses along.

He moved on very slowly, with his hands clenched in his pockets. It wouldn't do to go too fast, he wanted to give the cats time to come out into the front gardens. Let there be nine of them, he thought. And, Shall I ever find that book again? Or has it really vanished? Did I really see Madame Bonamy? Or was she just a dream? Can Mother and Father miss her as much as I do?

While he walked on up the hill—methodically noting the tortoiseshell at Number 19 and the Siamese at Number 12—two thoughts floated to the top of his mind and stayed there.

Perhaps Simon will be the ninth cat. And, Perhaps Father will have put on the kettle by the time I get back.

About the Authors

Norma Fox Mazer

grew up in Glens Falls, New York, in the foothills of the Adirondack Mountains, where her immigrant grandparents settled. Since her first book, *I, Trissy*, appeared in 1971, she has published many novels and two collections of stories. "I write every day," she reports, "in the same rhythm as I eat and sleep." *Taking Terri Mueller* (1981) and *Downtown* (1983) are suspenseful novels by Norma Fox Mazer. If you enjoyed "Tuesday of the Other June," you can find more of Norma Fox Mazer's short stories in *Dear Bill, Remember Me? and Other Stories* (1976) and *Summer Girls, Love Boys and Other Short Stories* (1982). Mazer's fine novel *After the Rain* (1987) was named a Newbery Honor Book.

Robert Cormier

worked for many years as a newspaperman before he turned to writing fiction full time. He learned to write, he says, by "constant reading, reading, reading." He explained in a *Horn Book* interview (May–June 1985): "I'm always asking as I read, 'How did the writer do this? Why do I suddenly have tears in my eyes?' " After publishing three novels for adults,

Mr. Cormier published his first book for younger readers, *The Chocolate War*, in 1974. That book, a chilling look at corruption and conformity in a high-school setting, is both thought-provoking and powerful. Readers' questions about what happened to the characters after the book's end led Mr. Cormier to write *Beyond the Chocolate War*, his fifth novel for young adults, published in 1985. If you liked the story "President Cleveland, Where Are You?" you may want to read the author's novel *Other Bells for Us to Ring* (1990) about a family of outsiders in Frenchtown. Robert Cormier is the recipient of the Young Adult Services Division *School Library Journal* Author Award, which recognizes authors "whose books have provided young adults with a window through which they can view their world and which will help them to grow and to understand themselves and their role in society."

Tricia Springstubb

says she never expected to be a writer, longing instead at different times to be a cowgirl, a nun, and an archaeologist. She has sold soap dishes and shower curtains and worked as a waitress and a teacher. She, too, learned to write by reading great writers. Books for young readers by Tricia Springstubb include *Give and Take* (1981), *The Moon on a String* (1982), and *Which Way to the Nearest Wilderness?* (1984). She has also published numerous short stories and articles for adults. You can find out more about Joy and

Eunice, the characters in "Last Summer," by reading *Eunice Gottlieb and the Unwhitewashed Truth About Life* (1987) and *Eunice (the Egg Salad) Gottlieb* (1988), also by Tricia Springstubb.

E. L. Konigsburg

is the only author whose work includes the Newbery Medal winner and a Newbery Honor Book of the same year. Those books were *From the Mixed-up Files of Mrs. Basil E. Frankweiler* and *Jennifer, Hecate, Macbeth, William McKinley, and Me, Elizabeth*, and the year was 1968. She started out as a chemistry teacher but switched to writing for young readers when she became more interested in the experiences of her students and her own children than in chemistry. Mrs. Konigsburg's books include two short story collections for children: *Altogether, One at a Time* (1971) and *Throwing Shadows* (1979). She lives in Florida, not far from a beach where sharks' teeth are carried ashore from a nearby fossil bed.

Lois Lowry

was born in Honolulu but went to college in New England, and now she divides her time between Beacon Hill in Boston and a 145-year-old farmhouse in New Hampshire. Her first book for young people was the poignant novel *A Summer to Die* (1977). Mrs. Lowry has written many other books, including a series of very funny ones about Anastasia Krupnik.

In 1990 her book *Number the Stars* received the American Library Association's Newbery Medal as the most distinguished children's book by a United States author. In this gripping novel, a young Danish girl helps Jewish friends escape from the Nazis.

Philippa Pearce

is the daughter of a flour miller whose mill stood on the river Cam in England. Her books *The Minnow Leads to Treasure* (1954), *Tom's Midnight Garden* (1958), and *A Dog So Small* (1962) are all set in that vicinity. After her education at Cambridge University, Philippa Pearce worked as a scriptwriter and producer for BBC radio, good preparation for a writer, she believes. *Tom's Midnight Garden* won the Carnegie Medal, England's equivalent of our Newbery Medal. Both this book and her novel *The Way to Sattin Shore* (1983) will appeal to you if you like stories with a bit of mystery in them. Additional short stories by Mrs. Pearce can be found in the collections *What the Neighbors Did and Other Stories* (1972) and—for those who enjoy spooky tales—*The Shadow Cage and Other Stories of the Supernatural* (1977).

Constance C. Greene

believes that even happy childhoods have their agonies and that it helps to be able to laugh at them and at oneself. She grew up in a family of newspaper people and always wanted to be a writer. The most thrilling day of her life, she says, was when she sold *A Girl Called Al* to Viking Press (1969). It was followed by *I Know You, Al* (1975), *Your Old Pal, Al* (1979), and *Al(exandra) the Great* (1982). Other funny and touching books she's written for young readers include *The Unmaking of Rabbit* (1972) and *The Ears of Louis* (1974). *Beat the Turtle Drum* (1976), a sadder book, is a favorite of many readers. *Star Shine* was published in 1985.

John Wideman

grew up in Pittsburgh and went on to the University of Pennsylvania, where he was an outstanding scholar and captain of the basketball team. He then won a Rhodes Scholarship to study in England. Professor Wideman has also lived in Wyoming and Massachusetts, but he discovered long ago that he writes best about the close African American community in which he grew up. One of his books for adults, *Sent for You Yesterday* (1983), won the PEN Faulkner Award. In his best-known book *Brothers and Keepers* (1985), John Wideman tries to understand how it happened that he grew up to be a college professor while his younger brother ended up serving a life sentence in prison. The books John Wideman has published so far have been written for adults, but he wrote the story "Shoes" for younger readers.

Joan Aiken

was born and grew up in England although her parents were American and Canadian. Her father, Conrad Aiken, was a distinguished poet. Joan was educated at home by her mother until she was twelve. She grew up listening to wonderful stories—reading aloud was a daily habit in her family—and by now she has written over fifty books herself. You perhaps know her rollicking novels *The Wolves of Willoughby Chase* (1963), *Black Hearts in Battersea* (1964), and *Nightbirds on Nantucket* (1966). (She won England's *Guardian* Award for these three books.) Joan Aiken has also published short stories for children, sad ones and funny ones, realistic stories and fantastic tales. Two good collections are *The Faithless Lollybird* (1978) and *Up the Chimney Down* (1985). *The Moon's Revenge* (1987) is an enthralling picture book for those of any age who love a satisfying tale, beautifully illustrated.

Elizabeth Segel

is codirector of Beginning with Books, a pioneering family literacy program affiliated with the Carnegie Library of Pittsburgh, which encourages parents and caregivers to read to children and supplies them with the necessary books to do so. She previously taught fiction and children's literature courses at the University of Pittsburgh, and from that experience she conceived the idea for this book. Dr. Segel is coauthor of *For Reading Out Loud! A Guide to Sharing Books with Children* (1983, 1988, 1991).